WW84

WONDER WOMAN DC

THE DELUXE JUNIOR NOVEL

Wonder Woman: The Deluxe Junior Novel
All rights reserved. Printed in the United States of America.
No part of this book may be used or reproduced in any manner whatsoever without written permission except
in the case of brief quotations embodied in critical articles and reviews. For information address HarperCollins
Children's Books, a division of HarperCollins Publishers, 195 Broadway, New York, NY 10007.
www.harpercollinschildrens.com
Library of Congress Control Number: 2019957956
ISBN 978-0-06-296335-2
Book design by Erica De Chavez
20 21 22 23 24   PC/LSCH   10 9 8 7 6 5 4 3 2 1
❖
First Edition

WW84

WONDER WOMAN DC

THE DELUXE JUNIOR NOVEL

ADAPTED BY:
Calliope Glass

SCREENPLAY BY:
Patty Jenkins
Geoff Johns
David Callaham

STORY BY:
Patty Jenkins
Geoff Johns

WONDER WOMAN CREATED BY:
William Moulton Marston

HARPER
An Imprint of HarperCollinsPublishers

PROLOGUE

Far from the world of man, hidden in an ocean of time, a lonely island shone in the sea like a steadfast emerald.

Themyscira.

It was the secret home of the legendary Amazons. These fearsome warriors had been created by Zeus to protect mankind from Ares, the god of war. With the last of his strength, the dying Zeus had hidden the Amazons away on Themyscira. There they waited, trained, and watched. One day Ares would return, and when that day came, they would be ready.

Once a year, the Amazons all gathered together in the huge stadium they had carved into the cliffside wall of the island. The Amazon Games.

Diana, the young princess of the Amazons, *lived* for the Games. And this year, for the first time ever, she was going to compete. Diana had been raised by her mother,

Hippolyta, the queen of the Amazons, to be always aware of her station.

A great, deep horn blew. The sound echoed over the cliffs of Themyscira. Diana could feel it in the soles of her feet. She took a deep breath and strode to the starting line. She dug her toes into the soft dirt and tried to calm the beating of her heart.

The race was about to begin.

Diana's aunt, Antiope, caught her eye. Antiope was Hippolyta's sister, and the commander of the Amazon army.

"I've seen the contest humble even the most seasoned of warriors, Diana," she told her niece.

Diana scowled. She would *prove* her aunt wrong. She would win the race. Then Antiope would see that she was a worthy competitor.

The herald standing by the starting line raised her giant mallet. It was time to focus. It was time to show everyone that she was ready to be one of the greats. She hunkered down, bracing herself, as the herald brought the mallet down on the huge gong.

BWAAAAAAMMMMMMMMMMMMMM.

With the sound of the gong crashing in her ears and buzzing in her teeth, Diana sprang into a sprint. The first leg of the race was an obstacle course. It was arguably the most exhausting part of the race, but Diana had watched the race her whole life, and she knew every bit of strategy. She knew it was vital to gain the lead early.

Diana ran as fast as she could, scrambling, jumping, and swinging from obstacle to obstacle. But her shorter legs meant she was easily outpaced by the adults she was competing with. By the time she was scaling a sheer wall close to the end of the obstacle course, she was already falling behind.

But she wasn't worried. Being small had its disadvantages, but it also had some major advantages that would come in handy later in the race. She just had to be patient. She leaped off the wall, landing neatly on one knee, and threw herself into a sprint to the next obstacle. This one was a long balance bar—a single log that spanned a deep pit. Another huge log, the same length, swung in a long arc just above it, hanging from two ropes. With each pass, the big log swept by the balance bar, about a foot above it.

Every Amazon in the race did her best to run the full length of the balance bar before the log swung back and knocked her off. But the balance bar was too long—it was just impossible to outrun the swinging log. And so

Amazon after Amazon was knocked into the pit, and forced to scale the steep walls of the pit before she could return to the race.

But not Diana. She began her run across the bar, and then, as the log swept down toward her, she threw herself down on the log and lay flat. She pressed her cheek to the rough surface of the balance bar and squeezed her eyes shut.

The wind ruffled her hair as the huge log swung by her . . . but it didn't touch her. Diana scrambled back up and sprinted the rest of the distance to the safety of the far side of the pit.

And now she was in the lead!

Diana ran full tilt toward the end of the obstacle course—a sheer drop down hundreds of feet into the ocean! She kicked off the edge of the cliff and fell, moving her body into a perfect arcing dive.

Splash! Diana knifed into the water, swerving up toward the surface as quickly as she could. As she swam toward shore, she heard the muffled *splash, splash, splash* of her fellow Amazons hitting the water behind her. She had the lead, but she couldn't afford to slow down.

Waiting on the beach was a string of gorgeous horses, tacked up and ready to run. Diana charged out of the water and leaped onto her horse, giving it a sharp tap with her heels. It sprang into a gallop, and as it ran she leaned over in the saddle and grabbed a waiting bow. There were arrows in a quiver strapped to the saddle. Without hesitating for a moment, Diana nocked an arrow on her bow and stood up in her saddle to steady herself against the jolting of her galloping horse. In one smooth motion, she drew the string, aimed, and shot.

Thump. She hit her first target squarely. A plume of colored smoke rose. Diana's plume was blue, while the other competing Amazons were assigned their own unique color. The idea was that when an Amazon struck a target, her smoke would rise high into the sky so the attendees in the stadium could see who was in the lead at a great distance.

Back in the stadium, the crowd cheered and her aunt and mother smiled with pride as the blue smoke rose high into the air.

Thump. Thump. Thump. Every arrow Diana fired found its target.

Diana guided her steed expertly, leaning forward as he leaped across deep gullies and swerved through dense forests. And as they galloped up the mountain, the other Amazons were never far behind.

Soon the path of the race swept along the side of the mountain, curving and heading back down the slope on a treacherous mountain road.

Sneaking a peek over her shoulder to see where the other racers were, Diana shifted her weight to the left just as her horse veered right. The world blurred and her stomach lurched as she sailed out of the saddle, hitting a tree branch with a bone-jarring thump.

Diana staggered to her feet. Her horse was unfazed, slowly coming to a stop a few paces ahead.

I want this, Diana thought. *I want to win. I want it so badly, so I can show everyone how strong I am despite being small.*

She watched as the other Amazons raced past her.

Diana couldn't give up. She began to sprint toward her horse and in one motion grabbed the reins and lifted herself back onto the saddle.

Diana hunched over her horse's neck as it lengthened its strides into the final sprint toward the stadium. Back in the stadium, they could see another target was hit in the distance . . . but Diana's color was nowhere to be seen. Her family was growing concerned.

Diana was in last place. But it didn't matter anymore.

She just needed to finish. She couldn't give up. Not now—not this close to the finish line. Her heart pounded jubilantly in her chest as she leaped from the saddle at the entrance to the stadium, to complete the race on foot, as was required.

The finish line was a large beaten-gold hoop hanging over the field. A line of spears were struck into the ground in front of the hoop. The spears loomed up and she slid by them, grabbing the one at the end of the line and heaving it into the air—

—Only to have her wrist caught in a viselike grip. Diana's momentum swung her around. She slid to her knees, undone by despair, as one of the Amazons ahead of her, who had once been hot on her tail, plucked a spear out of the ground and flung it through the shimmering golden hoop.

The crowd of Amazons thronging the stands leaped to their feet, roaring in jubilation.

Diana's whole body gave out. She had lost. She dangled like a puppet from the grip that was still firmly holding her wrist. Who—?

She looked up. Her aunt Antiope looked down at her steadily.

Diana dashed tears out of her eyes. When had she started crying?

"I wanted to win," Diana whispered.

"But you didn't," Antiope said, still so terribly gentle. "You cannot be the winner, little warrior, because you are not ready to win. And there is no shame in that. The only shame is in knowing the truth in your heart and yet still not accepting it. No true hero is born from lies."

She released Diana's wrist and gathered her into a gentle hug. Diana watched from her aunt's arms as the rest of the Amazon competitors gathered around the statue of the Fallen Hero in the center of the stadium. The Amazon in the statue stood proudly, her head held high. Her armor was shining gold, and a pair of magnificent stone wings sprang from her back.

"Your time will come, Diana," a voice said. Her mother's voice. Diana looked up as Hippolyta knelt down to face her. Hippolyta took Diana's face in her hands, staring deeply into her eyes. "When you are ready. Consider the Golden Warrior Asteria." She nodded toward the statue of the Fallen Hero. "She did not become a legend out of haste. She got there through acts of bravery . . . and the bravest thing of all is the courage to face the truth."

Hippolyta helped Diana stand. "One day you'll become all the things you dream of and more," she told her daughter. "And then everything will be different."

Everything will be different.

ONE

Everything was different.

Diana sighed as she looked out over the roofs of the city. Cars lurched their way through gridlocked intersections below. People bustled along the sidewalks, hurrying to work. The noise of TVs blaring in shop windows, cars honking their horns, and distant airplanes assailed her ears.

Everything in the Washington, DC, of 1984 was different. It was different from Themyscira, obviously. The concrete highways and scowling businessmen of Washington might as well have been a different world altogether from the cobblestones and warm smiles of Themyscira.

But it was worse than that: 1984 in Washington, DC, was also different from London in 1918. And the scowling businessmen could not have been further from the warm smiles of—

Diana shook her head. It was too easy for her to get lost in her memories of 1918 and . . . and Steve. Steve

Trevor, whose warm smile and shining eyes were the last things she thought of every night when she lay down to sleep, and the first thing she remembered every morning when she awoke. Steve Trevor, who had died. Had died saving the world, like the hero he was.

Diana had felt her heart break that day. She had thought, for a while, that she couldn't go on. But she'd gone on. What choice did she have? She was Earth's protector. Ordinary humans were so fragile. Their lives were so brief. It was her duty as an Amazon and a princess of Themyscira to protect them. And so she had.

She'd fought in two world wars. She'd battled crime on three different continents. She'd worked at various museums, using her knowledge of the classical world to get jobs. And she'd moved from city to city over the decades, doing what work she could to make peoples' lives safer, longer, and happier.

And if her own life wasn't very happy . . . well, Diana tried not to think about that very much. She lost herself in her work and her crime fighting, and she didn't make friends. She didn't want them, not after losing the first friends she'd made when she had entered the world of man in 1918. Those friends had all died, one by one, in the years and decades after World War I. Once the dust had settled and people were returning back to their normal lives after the war, she moved to the US with Etta. Diana was there for every one of her friend's birthdays, weddings, and funerals. Each loss had hit her harder. Each loss had left her more alone. Until, finally, she accepted her new life. Alone.

Diana smiled ruefully. She had caught herself straying into the past again—something that happened all too often. She needed to focus on *now*, on what was happening right in front of her eyes.

Crouched on the rooftop of a stately old bank, she looked out over Washington, DC. She used her sharpened Amazonian senses to listen for trouble. And then she heard it—tires screeching, someone screaming. A crash was about to happen. In a flash, Diana leaped from the building and bounded several blocks east. She slid into an intersection just as the screeching sports car was blowing through a red light. A jogger in sky-blue spandex tights and leg warmers was just turning to stare in horror at the car that was about to end her life.

Diana grinned as she moved—too fast for a human eye to track. She loved this part of the job. She slid in ahead of the sports car and got her shoulder under the fender. With a heave, she stopped the car and sent it sailing backward, away from the untouched jogger.

Then, faster than anyone could see, she raced away.

Diana had found, over the years, that she liked to work alone. Invisibly. It was easier that way. Easier to avoid getting involved, getting entangled. Just . . . easier.

It was a beautiful morning in DC. The air was warm and soft, and the sun filtered through the green leaves of the trees. The old stone buildings looked especially grand in the summer light. Diana stayed on the move, a blur that most people didn't even notice. She found herself enjoying the day, flitting from one near-disaster to another. She stopped a mugging, caught a woman falling off a bridge, rescued a kitten from a tree, and caught a baby's pacifier before it could hit the dirty ground.

Diana paused long enough to wink at the baby, who stared at her with wide eyes while his mother looked in the other direction, oblivious.

The baby's mother was watching a wall of TV screens in the window of an electronics store. They all showed the same man, talking. He had an eager smile on his face. It was a look that said, "Trust me."

"Life is good," the man was saying. "But it can be better. . . ."

Diana realized that she'd been hearing this man talking all morning—televisions all around DC were playing his commercial, and her finely tuned hearing had been picking it up everywhere she went.

"I'm Maxwell Lord," he went on. "And for a low monthly fee . . ."

Diana rolled her eyes. The man was charming, yes, but she had seen enough con men in her eighty years in the human world . . . she knew how to spot one a mile away. And Maxwell Lord was a con man if ever she'd seen one.

"Welcome to Black Gold Cooperative!" Maxwell Lord said earnestly on the television. "The world's first oil company run *for* the people, *by* the people. You can own a piece of the most lucrative industry in the world. And every time *we* strike gold, *you* strike gold."

Diana shook her head and hoped that not too many people would be taken in by whatever this man's scheme actually was.

She heard someone scream. Duty called.

Diana waved goodbye to the baby and leaped into the air.

The scream had come from a mall. When Diana plummeted out of the sky and landed lightly on the roof, she could hear the panicking crowd inside the mall without any trouble.

"Help!" someone was yelling. "They've got a hostage!"

Diana raised her fist and brought it down against the glass of a skylight.

Crash! Her fist shattered the window, and she leaped down into the central atrium of the mall. As she fell, she spotted a group of four rough-looking men—it was clearly a robbery gone wrong. They had a young girl as a hostage. Diana twisted and swerved as she fell, so that she landed right at the robbers' feet. With a move too fast for them to follow, she grabbed the hostage away from them. She leaped to safety with the young girl in her arms and deposited her gently on one of the coin-operated horse rides.

Then Diana leaped back to the robbers, flinging her tiara as she went. It bounced off the three security cameras she'd spotted, breaking them. *Good.* There wouldn't be a recording of this—Diana did what she could to avoid that. It was getting harder, in this age of television cameras and VCRs, but she was adaptable.

Diana alighted squarely in front of the four robbers. She stood, hands on her hips, and finally let them really see her. Her tiara was back on her head, keeping

15

her long black hair out of her face. The bracers on her wrists gleamed in the sickly fluorescent lighting of the mall. Her armor and boots were a nod to the ancient Greek styles worn in Themyscira. Diana looked like a warrior from a different place and time, and she knew it. She loved it—her costume allowed her to honor her home, and it also set her apart from the world of ordinary humans.

And, best of all, it frightened criminals.

Like the cowardly bunch that was now edging away from her. Diana grinned. This was going to be fun.

Two of the robbers ran in one direction, and the third and fourth dashed off the opposite way. Diana shrugged. This would be easy. She crouched, then jumped—a mighty leap that sent her bounding off the side of the wall of the mall atrium. With four more vertical strides along the walls, she landed in front of the first two robbers. They raised their fists, ready to fight! But Diana had studied boxing with the greatest warrior in the history of the world—Antiope. These petty criminals didn't stand a chance against her. She dodged in, fists tight, and battered them with a flurry of blows that were too fast for them to even see! Then, with two neat taps, she knocked the robbers right out.

Applause burst out from the crowd of shoppers watching the fight. Diana smiled and acknowledged them. But she wasn't done yet! The other two robbers were sprinting for the exit. Diana yanked her golden lasso off her hip and snapped it so it unfurled to its full length. With a flick of her wrist, she directed the shining golden cord so the end wrapped around a beam. Diana sprang out into the atrium and swung, the wind tugging at her hair, in a wide arc toward the fleeing robbers.

She landed with a light tap in front of them, and gave her lasso another flick to detach it from the chandelier. Then she swung it neatly around the robbers, tying them so tightly that they couldn't move.

When the police arrived at the mall, they found a crowd of onlookers all chattering excitedly about a mysterious woman—a hero who had saved the day. Who was she? Where had she come from? And where had she disappeared to?

They also found four robbers, neatly tied up with jump ropes from a nearby fitness store, staring sullenly at them from the very center of the atrium.

As Diana sailed across the rooftops of DC, she listened to the sounds of the city around her. Airplanes in the sky. Traffic on the streets. Dogs barking in parks. Babies crying in strollers. Typewriters and rotary phones in offices. And the high-pitched whine of TV screens in nearly every shop, nearly every home. Earlier that morning, nearly all of those televisions had been showing that man Maxwell Lord. Now they were mostly tuned to the news, and Diana heard, from a thousand televisions nearby, the news anchor say:

"Police and bystanders are reporting that the robbery was foiled by a 'mysterious female savior.' And if that sounds familiar, it should! There have now been half a dozen similar sightings across the greater DC area in the past year, causing some to call her the Woman of Wonder, and others to ask: Who *is* she, and where did she come from?"

Diana frowned. It might be time to move on soon. She had a nice job here in DC, working for the Smithsonian National Museum of Natural History. They knew her as Diana Prince, a curator specializing in the classical world. She enjoyed the work, and she liked DC. But she had learned that it was better not to get attached.

Better not to get . . . invested.

That night, back in her chic, modern apartment, Diana looked around her. Moving on wouldn't be hard. Her apartment was stylish, but it was also mostly empty. Diana traveled light, which meant she lived light too. She had a handful of souvenirs from World War I and World War II—photographs, mostly. Memories captured on yellowing photo paper. Etta. Chief. Charlie. Sameer. And . . .

And Steve.

Diana sighed. She picked up Steve's watch—her most treasured memento. The leather wristband was battered, the face was scuffed, and the hands were still. No quiet ticking could be heard. The watch was permanently stopped at 9:06 . . . the moment Steve had died.

Steve Trevor had been the first person Diana had met from the world outside Themyscira. His plane had crashed in the ocean near Diana's peoples' island, and she'd pulled him from the water. She'd dragged him onto the beach and watched his eyes flutter open— those thoughtful, perceptive blue eyes. And she hadn't known it at the time, but she'd fallen in love right then and there.

And now, all she had left of the love of her life was a broken watch.

Yes, she would be sure that Steve's watch came with her when she moved on . . . but for now, it would stay in her cold, empty apartment. And so would she.

Diana's stomach growled. Suddenly she was *famished*. She'd forgotten all about dinner! Normally Diana picked something up on her way home from work, but she'd gotten distracted by another one of those Maxwell Lord TV commercials on her way home, and she'd completely forgotten. Well, it wasn't a big deal. She could cook dinner for herself. Surely it wasn't that hard.

She opened her refrigerator door, and a cold blue light shone out.

"Let's see . . ." Diana murmured. Eggs. An old cauliflower. Some half-moldy cheese. And in the freezer, some iced-over frozen peas.

"Omelet it is," Diana said. She was a centuries-old demigod with superpowers and a magic lasso. She could definitely make an omelet.

Fifteen minutes later, she threw the windows open and released a black plume of smoke into the warm DC night air. The remains of her attempted omelet sizzled in the sink, blackened and smoking.

She could definitely not make an omelet.

Diana threw on a jacket and headed out the door. There was a nice restaurant on the corner—she'd just eat there.

"Excuse me, miss?" the waiter said. Diana looked up, startled. "Are you waiting for someone?" he continued, gesturing at the empty place setting across the table from her.

Diana shook her head. "No," she said. "Just me."

She ordered an omelet. It wasn't burnt. In fact, it was delicious. Diana smiled a bit as she ate—one of the nice things about the modern world was how easy it was to get a good meal that you didn't have to cook yourself.

The waiter removed the empty plate and the cutlery. Long after he'd left, Diana kept staring at the empty chair across from her. She was alone. But worse than that, she was adrift. Out of place.

She felt as if she no longer belonged.

TWO

Barbara Minerva didn't belong, and she knew it. She was too nervous. Too eager. Too nerdy. Too awkward. She'd been unpopular in high school. She'd been unpopular in college. Heck, she'd even been unpopular in graduate school, which took some doing. And now she was probably going to be unpopular at her new job.

But at least she was popular with her cat. Barbara squinted at her reflection in the bathroom mirror, gave her hair a final spritz of hair spray, and hurried into the kitchen, where her cat, Spot, was yowling for breakfast. Spot twined herself around Barbara's ankles as Barbara shook kibble into the bowl.

"There you go, sweetie," she said, scratching Spot behind the ears as the cat dug into her breakfast.

"And now," Barbara said, "time for *my* breakfast." She opened the fridge and peered in. Eggs, cheese, some vegetables—

"Perfect," she said. "Omelet it is."

Ten minutes later, Barbara was carefully sprinkling some chiffonaded parsley over a steaming, perfectly golden vegetable omelet.

I might be a flibbertigibbet, she thought ruefully as she dug in, *but I can definitely make an omelet.*

Barbara dressed with extra care. It was only her second week at this new job at the Smithsonian National Museum of Natural History. It was a big deal. It could be huge for her career, and she wanted to make a good impression. She chose an outfit that screamed "respectable businesswoman."

My battle armor, she thought as she carefully adjusted the high collar on her blouse.

On her way out the door, she waffled about her shoes.

"Heels or flats?" Barbara murmured. "Heels say, 'I kick butt' . . . but flats say, 'I probably won't *fall* on my butt if I wear these.'"

Barbara finally decided to split the difference. She put on a pair of tennis shoes for the walk to work, and changed into her very modest heels the moment she got to the museum.

Click, click, click. Barbara strode through the marble lobby of the natural history museum with her head held high and her shoulders back. This was more than a new job. This was a new *life* for Barbara Minerva. From now on, no more awkward nerd. No more nervous nobody. Starting today, Barbara Minerva was a confident, sophisticated, glamorous—

Splat. Barbara stepped wrong, turned an ankle, and went down like a ton of bricks. Her briefcase hit the floor with a crash, spilling papers everywhere.

Shoot.

Barbara sighed. Who was she kidding? She began shuffling her papers together and putting them back into her briefcase. People walked by, not stopping, not looking. She was grateful, really. That's what she told herself. She didn't want their help, didn't need it. She didn't want to make a scene. Nobody was helping her because nobody wanted to embarrass her by making a big deal of it, that was all. They were doing her a favor. They were being nice.

She almost believed it.

But when a beautiful woman with kind eyes knelt down and started to help Barbara with her papers, she didn't feel embarrassed at all. She felt grateful.

"Good morning," the woman said.

"Thanks," Barbara said, smiling shyly. "Hi . . ."

"Diana," the woman supplied. "I'm in cultural anthropology and archaeology."

"Barbara," Barbara answered. "Uh, geology, gemology, lithology, and cryptozoology. That last one's just for fun, though."

Diana raised her eyebrows. She looked impressed. Barbara smiled again. "I kept busy in school," she explained.

Diana smiled. She looked like she was ready to head off to whatever important meeting she'd doubtless been on her way to.

"Heels!" Barbara said a little frantically. "I was wearing these new heels, and—I know it's stupid. Heels are stupid. I just thought, it would be nice . . . What am I talking about? I'm a scientist. Scientists don't wear heels."

"Sometimes we do," Diana said.

"Of course!" Barbara said eagerly. "Hey, do you want to get lunch?"

Diana looked at her kind of blankly.

"Not right now, obviously," Barbara hurried to add, "but later? Later today?"

This was going . . . not great.

"I have a lot of work today," Diana said gently.

"Yeah," Barbara said, her shoulders slumping. "Me too."

"No," Diana said, "I truly—"

"Diana! Long time no see!" A voice rang out in the echoing lobby. Carol, the museum director, hurried over to them, a friendly smile on her face.

"Do you know a Barbara Minerva?" Carol asked Diana.

"That's me. Hi, Carol," Barbara said nervously. "We met . . . you hired me, actually."

Carol looked at Barbara. "Oh," she said in a much less excited voice. "Oh, Barbara. Hi. I have something for you, actually. I need help from a gemologist."

Barbara perked up. If she couldn't be popular, then at least she could be useful.

"The FBI is delivering some artifacts this afternoon," Carol explained. "They intercepted an undocumented ship full of them last night. Apparently the items were stolen and on their way to private buyers. But the FBI wants our help identifying one of them in particular."

The FBI? This was so cool! Barbara immediately began to imagine how awesome it was going to be. She would nail the identification, and they'd be so impressed by her that they'd offer her a job as an FBI agent right there on the spot! She'd get a badge and a partner, and before you knew it, she'd be breaking up smuggling rings, and eventually she'd be the head of the FBI, and the president would call her personally to tell her about his day, and—

Barbara realized she was just standing there and smiling. Carol was starting to look annoyed. So Barbara wiped the smile off her face and pasted on the most serious and respectable professional expression she could manage. "Of course," she said. "I'm happy to help."

That afternoon, Carol brought Barbara to a fancy new lab space. Other museum employees milled around, working on their various projects. But there, on one of the tables, were several items laid out just for Barbara. What fun! Mysterious treats from the FBI! Barbara bustled over to the table, grabbed a notepad and a tape recorder, and got to work.

"Item number twenty-three is . . . ," Barbara murmured into her tape recorder. It was several hours later, and she was still deep in the assignment. She'd been able to identify a bunch of the artifacts, but this one was going to be tricky. She squinted at it, then picked up a jeweler's loupe for a closer look.

Nope, nothing. She had no idea.

"Ah, the Empress of Spain," a voice said behind her. Barbara jumped a mile. Diana leaned in next to her.

"Originally found on the wreck of the *Nuestra Señora de Atocha*," Diana continued. Barbara smiled. How cool was this lady? She knew everything.

"I couldn't resist coming to see," Diana said. "What's left?"

"Just this," Barbara said, moving on to the final item. Number twenty-four. She hoped it would be something really cool. Plus, maybe something that would impress Diana.

Barbara opened the box. Inside lay a yellow stone set in an ornate metal ring.

"Huh," Barbara said, disappointed. She'd been hoping for something spectacular, but this was just boring.

"What is it?" Diana asked, leaning over to see.

"I think the technical term would be 'extremely lame,'" Barbara quipped. "It's citrine. It's basically a fake gem. It's been used in fakes throughout history. It isn't valuable—this one looks like it might be pretty old, so it's probably worth . . . I don't know, maybe seventy-five dollars."

Diana looked thoughtful. "Fakes aren't my forte," she said, "but may I take a look?" Barbara nodded, and Diana lifted the stone out of its crate and turned it over in her hands, peering at it carefully. Barbara looked where she was looking—there was some kind of inscription on the gold ring set around the gem. It looked like Latin.

". . . place upon the object held . . . but *one* great wish . . . ," Diana murmured.

Incredible. "You can read *Latin*?" Barbara said. Was there anything Diana *couldn't* do?

"Languages are a hobby," Diana said modestly.

"One great wish, huh?" Barbara said thoughtfully. "So, like, a lucky charm."

One of the other museum workers overheard that as he walked by. Roger. Barbara had met him at orientation. He laughed and reached out to touch the stone. "I wish I had some coffee," Roger told it, smirking.

Barbara laughed too. But suddenly, out of nowhere, a woman appeared holding two paper cups of coffee. "I've got an extra," she said. "Anyone want it?"

Roger, Diana, and Barbara stared at each other. Well. That was bonkers timing! They burst into laughter.

"Sure," Roger said, "I'll take it! It's my greatest wish, after all." He grabbed the coffee and took a sip—then yelped in pain!

"Hot hot hot!" he said, running off to the cold water in the water cooler.

Barbara muffled her laughter as he went. She felt bad, but it was still hilarious. She looked over at Diana and found her new friend with a merry smile lighting up her face as well.

They both looked down at the yellow stone. The so-called wish-granting stone.

"Can you even imagine?" Barbara said. Diana's smile turned wistful.

"If only," she said. There was something sad about her voice.

"The worst thing is," Barbara confessed, "I don't even know what I would wish for."

Diana looked solemnly at the stone in her hand. She closed her eyes briefly. A soft breeze stirred Barbara's hair. She shivered.

"I do," Diana said. "I know." She sighed, and carefully put the yellow gem back in its box.

Barbara watched as Diana visibly came back to herself, putting on a pleasant, professional face. She smiled politely at Barbara and stood up to leave.

No, Barbara thought. *No, you don't.* She'd seen the real Diana there for a moment—a woman with regrets. Someone more complicated than just another perfectly poised professional woman. Barbara wanted to get to know the real Diana.

"Listen," she said awkwardly. "Thanks for, you know, for talking to me." *Ugh, that was so dumb,* Barbara thought. She winced.

But reaching out actually seemed to have an effect. Diana nodded thoughtfully. "How about we go get a drink?" she said. "We can talk about exactly how terrible that fake is."

Barbara beamed. "Right? So dumb!"

They walked out arm in arm. "Citrine," Diana said scornfully. "Who are they kidding?"

Barbara was so happy. She had a new friend—*and* her new friend was someone she could make gemology jokes with! Things were looking up.

In the chilly silence of Diana's Watergate apartment, Steve Trevor's watch sat motionless. Dead. And then, as though it had never stopped, it began to tick again after sixty-six years.

Tick.

The second hand clicked forward.

Tick.

The sound was shockingly loud in the quiet apartment.

Tick.

But nobody was there to hear it.

THREE

Diana liked Barbara. It sort of surprised her. These days, she was so disconnected. She had forgotten what it was like to speak to someone like you would speak to a friend. Talking to Barbara was easy. And more—it was fun.

". . . and that's when I found Spot!" Barbara was saying, wrapping up a story about her cat. "He was sitting next to the phone, listening to that voice that tells you the time of day!" She made a funny catlike face—and for a moment, she really *looked* like a cat.

Diana burst out laughing. "You're so funny!" she told Barbara. Barbara smiled bashfully as the waiter took their plates away. It had been a lovely night so far—a drink that had turned into dinner as the two new friends got to know each other.

"Well," Barbara said. "That's sort of the one thing I have going for me." She shrugged. "I like making people happy."

Diana put her hand over Barbara's. "Nobody's made me laugh in . . . I don't know how long. So thank you." She sighed. "I don't actually get out much, socially."

Barbara's eyes widened. "You?" she said. "You seem like the kind of person who would be really popular." She shook her head. "Me, I've never been popular. I've never even been *semi*popular."

Diana felt so confused. How could this sweet, funny, smart woman not be popular? Diana had liked her from the moment they'd met in the lobby of the museum. There was something about Barbara—she didn't hide anything. She was so frank, so open.

"But you're so personable," Diana protested. "So free. I must say, I envy that."

Barbara looked incredulous. "You envy *me*?" she said. "But you're so confident and strong." She made a muscle-arm gesture. Diana laughed. "No, seriously!" Barbara went on. "You look like you were carved out of marble by, like, Michelangelo or something!"

Not by Michelangelo, no, Diana thought. Barbara could never know how close her casual comment had come to the truth. Diana had been created by Zeus himself, not by mortal means.

Barbara went on. "People think I'm weird," she said. "They avoid me. They say things about me behind my back when I can still hear them." Her mouth twisted and she looked down at the table. "Sometimes I stay late at work just—"

"Just so you don't have to go home," Diana filled in. She knew *that* feeling very well. Loneliness.

Barbara looked up, astonished. As though it had never occurred to her that Diana might not have a perfectly happy life.

Diana fumbled for the right words. How to explain without explaining? Barbara could never know the truth about Diana, obviously, but still, she wanted to share *something* true with her.

"Barbara," she started, choosing her words carefully, "my life . . . it hasn't been what you probably think it has." If only Diana could tell her about Themyscira. About World War I. About . . . about Steve. *All* about Steve. But she could never. "We all . . . we all have our struggles," she finished softly.

But Barbara looked comforted as well as confused. "So you of all people . . . ," she started. Then she veered into unexpected territory. "Have you ever been in love?" she blurted out.

The question was like a knife. In a flash, Diana's heart and head were filled with memories of Steve—his teasing smile, his strong hands. The smell of his leather jacket, and the way the wind ruffled his thick sandy hair just so. How quiet his voice could be. How he'd understood her so well from the first day. His bravery—the bravery that had been the death of him, as he piloted a stolen plane full of deadly chemical weapons into the sky so that, when it detonated, nobody was killed . . . except him.

How could she explain Steve? She couldn't. But she'd never stopped loving him. And his death had never stopped hurting her.

"Yes," Diana said after a moment, when her poor aching heart started beating again. "A long time ago." She turned the tables on Barbara. "You?"

Barbara nodded miserably. "Lots of times," she said. "So many times." Diana could tell from how she said it that none of those loves had ended happily.

Barbara tilted her head. "Where'd he go?" she asked innocently. "Your guy?"

"Well," Diana said plainly, "he died." Barbara's eyes went wide. And despite herself, Diana found herself telling Barbara more about Steve—how he once chased a squirrel thirty blocks in London because it had stolen his sandwich, laughing the whole way. How he'd spent an afternoon trying to teach her how to yodel. How he used to make puppets out of dinner napkins and make them say the most ridiculous things to each other.

"He thought he was so funny," Diana said, but she was laughing herself now, and so was Barbara.

They smiled at each other. "You've never loved again?" Barbara asked, her smile turning bittersweet.

Diana shook her head. "No," she said. "But it's okay. I don't really—"

In the distance, a siren wailed. It was far enough away that Barbara probably couldn't hear it. But Diana, with her divinely enhanced senses, could. And it meant she was needed. Wonder Woman was needed.

"I should go," Diana said, standing up in a hurry. Barbara nodded and grabbed her to-go boxes. They walked out together.

"Let's do it again sometime," Barbara said eagerly, and Diana found herself nodding.

"I'd like that," she said. "I really would." It had been a long time since Diana had had . . . a friend. Maybe it was time for her to put some of her old hurts behind her, at last. Maybe it was time to move on, and to find new connections in the world. New reasons to care.

Maybe.

Barbara was walking on air. What an evening! The food had been great, and Diana was—Diana was amazing. So smart, so sophisticated. But not at all snobby or standoff-ish—Barbara could tell that Diana really *liked* her. Diana had said they should get together again. Were they really going to become friends? It didn't seem possible.

It wasn't that Barbara had low self-esteem. Not exactly. She knew that she was very, very smart. She knew that she was kind, and loyal. She knew that she knew more than most people about a very wide variety of topics. But she also knew that smart, loyal know-it-alls weren't everybody's idea of a good time. Barbara could get nervous, she could be awkward. She often said the wrong thing.

Sometimes when she was getting ready for work, she felt more like a little kid dressing up like a grown-up than a confident professional woman wearing her own clothes.

Over the years, Barbara had learned that lots of people she would like to be friends with . . . didn't want to be friends with her. She tried not to dwell on it. But sometimes it was hard. She wished she was like Diana—beautiful, sophisticated, confident. Someone who turned heads. Someone everyone wanted to be near.

But Diana really seemed to *like* her.

Then Barbara forgot all about Diana for a moment. She'd spotted the person she'd been hoping to see on her walk home: Leon, a homeless man she'd befriended earlier that year.

"Hey there, Barbara!" Leon said. He waved from the park bench where he usually hung out. "Late night?"

Barbara smiled and hurried over. She held out the bag with her take-out boxes. She always made sure to order extra for Leon when she ate out.

"Late night," she agreed. "But I wanted to give you this while it was still warm."

Leon peered into the bag and sniffed appreciatively. "You're too good to me," he said, giving her a broad grin.

"It's no problem, Leon," Barbara said. She waved goodbye. "See you soon!"

Barbara cheerfully strode off. She liked Leon. He was a good listener, and a sweet guy. She was glad that she could be helpful to him here and there.

Barbara hummed a cheery tune as she walked. The DC streets were dark, but the air was still warm. She strode along, thinking happily about all the things she and Diana had talked about at dinner. But then—

"Hey there," a man's voice rasped from the dark. Barbara jumped. But she didn't turn, and she didn't stop walking. It was a man sitting on a bench by the sidewalk. Barbara could see him out of the corner of her eye, but she didn't want to turn to face him. She walked faster.

The man stood up and started walking next to her. *Oh geez,* Barbara thought. That was the last thing she wanted. She started walking even faster.

Then the guy grabbed her. But in that moment everything turned upside down. There was a big jolt, and suddenly she was flying through the air, flailing and twisting, trying to get her feet under her before she hit the ground. Time seemed to slow down as she desperately struggled to orient herself, and then—

Thump.

Barbara came to rest in someone's arms, unhurt. That someone gently put her down, feet first, and she stood shakily on the sidewalk, staring in astonishment at—

"Diana?"

Diana Prince smiled cheerfully at Barbara. She didn't have a hair out of place—she looked like she rescued helpless women from muggings every day. Heck, maybe she did.

Barbara shook her head. Where had the scary guy gone? She looked around. The sidewalk was empty except for the two of them. Then she spotted him—a crumpled heap against a trash can about thirty feet away.

"What—?" Barbara started.

"What was I doing in the area?" Diana said. She shrugged. "I forgot my keys at the restaurant."

"How—?" Barbara started again. She was having trouble wrapping her head around this entire situation.

"How did I take him down?" Diana filled in. "Simple self-defense. I used his own momentum against him. I'll teach you how, if you like. It doesn't take much power."

That didn't sound right to Barbara, but it also wasn't the first thing on her mind at the moment. The main thing was—

"Ugh," Barbara said, burying her face in her hands. "I'm so embarrassed."

"Why?" Diana said.

"I'm such a loser!" Barbara moaned. She couldn't *believe* how stupid she'd been. "I should have known better than to take this route. At *night. Alone.*" God, how could she have been so dumb?

Diana put her arm around Barbara. They started walking together toward the main avenue, where there was more light—and more people.

"Another day," Diana was saying. "Another place . . . and it would have been *you* helping *me.*"

That didn't sound right to Barbara either. Diana seemed like someone who could *really* take care of herself. But she didn't say anything.

Diana walked Barbara home and squeezed her hand gently at the door to the apartment building. "Get some sleep tonight," she said.

"Sure," Barbara said brightly. "Of course!" It sounded insincere even to her ears. But Diana only smiled and walked off, striding purposefully in those stiletto heels. Barbara sighed. She'd never be that cool. Never be that polished.

Spot meowed and twined her body around Barbara's feet when she walked in her front door. The apartment was dim and quiet. The digital clock on her bedside alarm glowed a soft red, and a cool breeze from an open window rustled her spider plants.

Barbara didn't bother turning on the lights as she bustled around, feeding Spot and tidying up for the night. She didn't really need the light, and she didn't particularly want to catch a glimpse of herself in any mirrors—she was tired of looking at her own face. Why couldn't she look more like Diana? Why couldn't she be strong and fearless like Diana?

After lying in bed staring at the ceiling for an hour, Barbara finally gave up. There was no way she was going to get to sleep anytime soon. She was still too rattled from the attack, and still too humiliated about her own helplessness. *I hate him,* she thought, remembering the horrible man who had grabbed her wrist as she walked home. *And I hate myself too.*

Barbara was tired of the way her thoughts were spinning around in her head. She sighed and got up to head back to the office. So it was one in the morning; so what? If she wasn't going to sleep, she could at least get some work done.

When Barbara arrived at the lab, the first thing she spotted was the box with article number twenty-four in it—the citrine with the bogus promise of wish granting inscribed on its setting. On an impulse, Barbara snatched it out of the box and carried it into her office.

She flopped down into her chair and glared at the dumb fake rock in her hand.

"I know what I would wish for," she muttered. She held it tight. "I'd wish to be like Diana. Strong. Cool. Beautiful. *Special.*"

For a moment Barbara didn't move, didn't breathe. For a moment it seemed like maybe the usual rules of the universe wouldn't apply. That physics and chemistry and cause and effect would somehow be temporarily set aside. That magic would turn out to be real.

For a moment, it seemed like somehow a citrine could actually grant a wish. Could actually make Barbara into something she wasn't—could *give* her something.

Something she wanted desperately.

Barbara squeezed her eyes shut.

And then—

Nothing happened.

Nothing, except a chilly breeze ruffled her hair and sent a shiver down her spine.

"Whatever," Barbara muttered, trying to pretend she wasn't disappointed. "It's kid stuff anyway."

She put the stone back on her desk and sat in the dark, alone.

Always alone.

Tick.

Diana lay in the dark, alone, staring at the ceiling. Her apartment was quiet and empty.

Tick.

She sighed, turned over in bed, and drifted off to sleep.

Tick.

In the next room, unnoticed, Steve Trevor's watch ticked, keeping perfect time after sixty-six years.

Tick.

Across town, a man opened his eyes and looked around.

Tick.

He had no idea where he was. He had no idea *when* he was.

Tick.

What was going on?

Tick.

What had happened to him?

FOUR

Barbara woke up with her face mashed into the keyboard of her word processor. Sunlight was streaming in through her office window, brutally bright.

"Mmrph," she moaned, and heaved herself up to sit upright. She'd fallen asleep in her office at some point, and now it was morning. The clock read 8:54. Muffled voices were audible in the hallway—people were already arriving at work. And here she was with QWERTY stamped backward into her cheek.

"Oh no," she muttered. She was still wearing yesterday's outfit. And now it was pretty crumpled. Barbara grabbed her gym bag from under her desk. Rummaging around, she found nothing really helpful. Instead, she took off her skirt and pulled her long sweater down, making a sort of sweater dress. Then she pulled one shoulder off to make it trendy. For some reason, today she felt like she could pull off a slightly cooler look. It wasn't perfect, but it was enough to disguise that she was still totally wearing the same clothes as yesterday. Whatever. It was fine.

It's not like anybody ever actually looks at me anyway, Barbara thought ruefully as she grabbed her makeup bag and headed for the bathroom.

"Looking good, Barbara!" someone said in the corridor.

For a moment, Barbara thought, *There must be another Barbara working at the museum.* And then she realized that her coworker Jake was talking to *her.* He gave her a friendly smile and a wink and went on his way.

That was weird, Barbara thought. Jake had completely ignored her until now. But then she caught a glimpse of herself reflected in a window. She *did* look good. Weirdly good.

Clonk. A janitor mopping up nearby knocked over his bucket of dirty soapy water, and a mini tidal wave came slooshing in Barbara's direction. Without thinking, she leaped over the stream of water, landing lightly on a chair in her high heels.

"Yikes," the janitor said. "Sorry!"

"No problem," Barbara said, smiling. None of the water had even touched her. That was cool—she wasn't usually that coordinated.

"Barbara!" a voice called from down the hall.

Carol—Barbara's new boss—was hurrying over to her. There was a man with her. He looked familiar. Barbara squinted at him, trying to place his face. He had auburn hair and dark eyes. Something about him seemed both kind and confident—the sort of man you'd trust with your kids. Or with your money.

"I wanted to introduce you to someone," Carol said, gesturing at the guy. He stuck out his hand, and Barbara shook it automatically. His hand was warm, and his handshake was firm and reassuring.

"It's a pleasure," he said with a charming smile.

"Do I know you?" Barbara asked, smiling back. "You look so familiar!"

"Do it! Do the thing," Carol said, nudging him.

The man smiled bashfully. "You got me," his expression said. Then he straightened and put on a serious face. *"Life is good,"* he said with a dramatic flourish, *"but it can be better!"*

"Oh!" Barbara said. Now she remembered—this guy's ads had been playing on TV for weeks now. "The oil guy from TV!" His name was . . . Maxwell King or something. Oh! Maxwell Lord. That was it.

"The oil guy, huh?" Maxwell Lord said, smiling that

charming smile. "Hey, I'll take it."

Carol took Lord's arm. "Mr. Lord here is considering becoming a *friend* of the Smithsonian," she told Barbara. *"At the partner level."* She delivered the last bit with considerable emphasis. Barbara had worked for enough institutions like the Smithsonian to know what that meant: *This guy has a ton of money, and he might give us a bunch of it.*

". . . Which entitles him to a handful of private tours of our facilities!" Carol concluded, with a chipper smile. She beamed at Barbara. "And he asked for *you* in *particular.*"

"Me?" Barbara said, baffled. *Why?*

"What can I say, Dr. Minerva?" Lord said. He winked. "Your reputation precedes you. We share a passion for gemology."

Carol backed off, waving her hands encouragingly at Barbara as she retreated behind Maxwell Lord.

"Oh," Barbara said awkwardly. "Well, cool." She took Maxwell Lord's arm and started walking toward her office. "Let me just set this down," she said, waving her makeup bag. When they got to her office, Barbara ducked inside, tossing her makeup bag onto a chair. She turned around, and—

"Yikes!" Maxwell Lord was *right there*. He was looking around her office with a lot of interest. Barbara's office was pretty boring, and it was also a *mess*. She didn't really want a potential partner-level friend of the Smithsonian, or whatever they called someone that rich, seeing how messy her office was.

"I, uh, didn't hear you follow me in," Barbara explained. She tried to usher him out. But his eyes were locked on her desk. What was on her desk that was so interesting? Barbara glanced over. She had a crystal paperweight, a messy stack of files, a dictionary, the word processor that had served as her pillow last night, and the citrine "wish-granter" fake that she and Diana had been giggling over. The one she'd tried to wish on last night. Barbara blushed. That had been so dumb. Who believed in *wishes*? Little kids. And sad adults, she supposed.

But Maxwell Lord was staring hungrily at the stone. Weird.

Barbara shooed him out of her office without much trouble, though, and brought him to the lab where she did most of her real work. Her little impromptu tour felt awkward at first, but Maxwell turned out to be a really sweet guy, and easy to talk to. By the time Diana came in, Barbara and Maxwell were laughing like old friends.

"Diana!" Barbara exclaimed, waving her new friend over. She couldn't wait to show off for Diana. She'd never believe who Barbara had been talking to this whole time. "I'd like you to meet . . ." Barbara did a cute little flourish with her arms, a *ta-da!* gesture revealing Maxwell Lord. "Maxwell!"

Maxwell grinned and extended his hand. Diana shook it but didn't smile. She looked a little confused.

Maxwell grinned bashfully. "Life is good," he prompted. Everyone had heard those words from his commercial a billion times. "But it can be better."

Diana still looked blank.

"From TV," Barbara whispered.

"Ah," Diana said. She gave Maxwell a sharp look. "Yes, I see now."

She didn't smile. Maxwell looked a little deflated.

Barbara shifted nervously. This wasn't going as well as she'd hoped. Diana glanced at her and seemed to realize the awkwardness.

"I don't have a TV," Diana explained to Maxwell apologetically. He brightened up.

"You know," Maxwell said helpfully, "I have a great relationship with Sears. I could have a brand-new set delivered to you by the end of the day. Nineteen inches! No strings attached."

Diana smiled politely. "I'll stick with the one I don't have, thank you," she said. Maxwell looked crestfallen again. Barbara winced. Diana wasn't helping at all! On the other hand, Barbara realized, she had no idea why Maxwell was so important to the museum. So Barbara hurried to interject.

"Diana, Maxwell was touring the *entire Smithsonian* while considering a partnership, but guess what he's just decided? To make the donation directly to *our* museum! He's announcing it at tonight's quarterly members' gala!"

She laughed in delight and squeezed Maxwell's arm. He grinned back at her, and Barbara's stomach fluttered a bit. He was really handsome! You couldn't tell on TV. But in real life—yikes!

Diana nodded solemnly. "I tend to skip these events," she said. "I find that our benefactors with a *true* eye toward philanthropy prefer to stay out of the spotlight. To let the museum's work garner the attention."

Barbara scowled at Diana. Why was she being such a snob? So Maxwell wanted to enjoy the spotlight a little. So what?

"Of course, of course," Maxwell said. He smiled

warmly at Diana. "But I do so love a party! And I assure you, the spotlight is the least of my interests here."

There! Barbara thought. *See?*

"That's very reassuring, Mr. Lord 'from TV,'" Diana said coldly. She glanced at Barbara. "Back to work then, Barbara?" she said, turning toward the door. Barbara started to follow her automatically, then hesitated. "Yes," she said. "But—"

She didn't really want to say goodbye to Maxwell. Not yet.

Maxwell grabbed her hand and gave it a gallant kiss.

"So lovely to meet you, Mr. Lord," Barbara said breathlessly.

"See you tonight," he replied, and strolled out of the lab.

Barbara was so flustered that she couldn't get her breath back enough to speak until he was already gone. "Bye," she said to nobody in particular. Then she looked up and caught Diana glaring at the empty doorway.

"What is it with you?" Barbara demanded. "How can you not think he's amazing?" She looked down at her crumpled, day-old outfit. No *way* was she going to wear this to the gala that night. "Oh gosh," she muttered. "I need some—"

Barbara didn't even bother to finish the sentence. She made a break for her office, grabbed her purse, and hurried off for some emergency shopping.

Back at the lab, Diana looked around thoughtfully. Nothing seemed to be out of place here. Maxwell Lord didn't seem to have disturbed any of the exhibits or artifacts that were currently being worked on. But he had obviously had some reason for coming to the museum. And Diana didn't buy for a second that the reason had anything to do with charitable intentions. He was after something.

But what?

A gleaming black luxury sedan pulled up in front of an opulent office building with a sparkling gold sign that read BLACK GOLD COOPERATIVE. The car's engine purred contentedly as it idled. A door opened with a soft *click*, and Maxwell Lord stepped out, smiling up at the building that represented his oil-fueled empire.

He closed the door behind him and patted the hood of the car twice to signal his driver to go on without him, then turned and strode confidently into the building. The lobby was all marble and gold—quiet and cool, as state-of-the-art industrial air-conditioning kept every-thing perfectly chilly in the summer heat. Maxwell loved this lobby. He'd put careful thought into every single design element, from the massive framed photographs that covered the walls, to the oil derrick sculpted out of gold adorning one corner of the echoing lobby. The overall effect was one of overwhelming prosperity—an untouchable, unsinkable business lived here. Maxwell took a moment to enjoy it before he braced himself and headed for the frosted glass doors at the back of the lobby.

"Mr. Lord!" Raquel, his secretary, called as she hur-ried up to him, her high heels clicking on the immaculate marble floor. She had a handful of envelopes in her hand. Maxwell winced. Bills, probably.

"Not now, Raquel," he said brusquely, and pushed his way through the doors into the part of the building nobody was supposed to see. The part where the *real* Black Gold Cooperative lived.

The real Black Gold Cooperative, a.k.a, a hollowed-out shell of a company. A noncompany. A big, fat lie.

The emperor's nonexistent new clothes.

The back office of Black Gold was completely empty.

Maxwell Lord sighed as he crossed the eerily silent office floor. Forget about workers—there weren't even empty cubicles. It was just a huge, echoing nothingness, with some wires sticking out of the ceilings and some phones on empty tables, waiting for furniture to sit on. Waiting for workers to pick them up and use them to make deals with. Waiting.

Waiting for a boom that was never coming.

Black Gold had looked so good on paper. Maxwell had had a *vision*. A *business plan*. He was going to revolutionize moneymaking. He was going to be swimming in wealth, and his investors were too. They'd spent a fortune on advertising. They'd shot lavish advertorials and blasted the airwaves with them nonstop. The whole world knew about Maxwell Lord. He had investors but couldn't deliver on his promises and owed people a lot of money. The venture was about to bust up, and Maxwell was about to be the biggest failure the world had ever seen—and flat broke, to boot.

He was desperate.

Maxwell swept into his office—the only actual office in the entire space. He took a deep breath as he slammed the door closed behind him. His last sanctuary. Finally, he was alone.

"It's over, Maxwell," a rough voice said. Maxwell jumped a mile and spun to face his desk. Simon Stagg, his biggest investor, was sitting in Maxwell's chair behind his desk, flipping dismissively through Maxwell's treasured collection of books on mythological artifacts. It had been the work of Maxwell's lifetime to amass that library of ancient texts. And Stagg was handling them as though they were trash. Maxwell felt his hackles go up. But he forced a smile onto his face. He couldn't afford to fight with Stagg. He needed him too badly.

"This office isn't ready for guests yet," he said pleasantly.

"It's over," Stagg said again. He tossed a book aside like it was an old magazine. *The Divine and Destructive Weapons of the Gods*—one of the most important texts Maxwell had come across in his research. The book that had led him to the . . . He hastily put the thought out of his head and scrambled to grab the book and set it upright before the binding could be damaged.

"I'm out," Stagg said.

Maxwell shook his head. He couldn't accept that. "I know it's hard to see, Simon," he said coaxingly, "but we are *finally* right at the edge of turning this thing around."

"Turning it around?" Stagg said, standing up and slamming his hands down on Maxwell's desk. "There's *no oil*! There never was!"

Maxwell's nerve broke. This was a disaster. Without Stagg, everything was going to fall apart. "N-no!" he protested. "I have a big . . . something's in the works! It's—"

He took a deep breath to steady his voice. "It's going to work, Simon," Maxwell said, as calmly as he could. "We have millions of acres of potentially oil-rich land."

Stagg sneered. "You have *oil rights* on land that everyone else has *already passed on*." Maxwell felt his stomach drop. Stagg wasn't supposed to know that. How had he—?

"You talk a big game," Stagg went on, his face turning red with fury, "but you're nothing but a low-life con man. You have forty-eight hours to get my money—"

"You're going to regret this," Maxwell said in a shaking whisper. Something wild and desperate was building inside him. He felt like his knees might give out. He felt like he might tear out Stagg's jugular with his actual teeth.

"—or the Federal Trade Commission is getting an anonymous report," Stagg finished. He stormed out.

The door to Maxwell's office slammed behind him.

FIVE

The National Museum of American History glittered in the DC night like an ancient jewel. Sleek, dark limousines lined up in front of it as Washington's elite arrived for the annual fundraising gala.

Diana glided through the crowd, feeling a bit like a fish swimming through a tank of sharks. Sharp smiles and sharper laughter surrounded her. She hated the gala. It was supposed to be a fundraising event for the museum—a very worthy cause indeed. But the people who attended were the kinds of people who wanted to be seen giving. Who gave in order to be seen. Everything in Washington, DC, was political, Diana had learned. Even charity. Especially charity.

"Hello, gorgeous," a man said, stepping in front of her and cutting her off. Diana neatly sidestepped him and continued on her way. She was looking for a man, yes, but not this man. Tonight she was looking for

Maxwell Lord. And he would not be happy when she found him.

Ah! There he was. Diana had spotted Lord making his way through the crowd, on the other side of the echoing room. He vanished as she pushed into the crowd, but Diana spotted him again, heading up the stairs. Then a waiter drifted into her line of sight and she lost him again.

"Hey there," another man said, stepping in front of her. Diana turned on him with a snarl.

"No, thank you," she said sharply, trying to be as polite as she could. She was seething with frustration. All she wanted was to track down Maxwell Lord and find out what he was up to—she was sure it was nothing good, and she was worried her friend Barbara was going to get caught up in it somehow. But all of these—these *gadflies*—kept getting in her way. Diana dodged past him and continued pushing toward the stairs.

"Diana!" called yet another man *who was not Maxwell Lord*. "I was hoping I'd see you!"

Diana didn't even bother looking at him. She just kept walking. But this guy fell into step next to her, hurrying along as she made her way to the stairs.

"Hey," he said, apparently not concerned that she'd failed to reply or even to look at him. "Did you know I'm at the White House now? That's right! I'm interning. But I was requested by name, you know? Listen, I've had my eye on you for a while. You're really going places! Or you can be, with the right friends. If you ever—"

Diana glanced at him, finally. "I'm busy, Carl," she said. "Thank you."

She swept up the stairs, finally alone. But Lord had definitely vanished.

Diana paused on the balcony. Where had he gone? Most of the museum was blocked off for the evening— they didn't want partygoers and donors wandering the archives unaccompanied. But there were a few rooms off the balcony that had been temporarily converted into quiet bar areas.

Choosing one of them at random, Diana opened a door and slipped in. The bar was dimly lit with small, glittering lights like stars. The roar of the crowd out in the main lobby space was suddenly muted as the door closed behind her—and yet another man slipped in just as it closed.

"Diana," he said. Diana glanced over. It was too dark to recognize if she knew him, and she was too

preoccupied to care. Another Carl, she supposed—
another small-time Washington ladder climber who
thought she could get him up another rung. She
wasn't interested in either option. And Maxwell Lord
wasn't here, which meant she wasn't going to be stay-
ing, either.

She swept by the man, heading for the door.

"Diana," the man said again, turning to follow her
back out.

Diana froze. "Steve?"

Earlier in the day, Barbara Minerva did something she
had never done before. She had gone to the mall to buy a
new dress to wear to the museum gala, and she'd spotted
a pair of high heels covered in bold crystal embellish-
ments. Encouraged by an eager saleswoman and maybe
a twinkle of newfound confidence, Barbara found herself sitting in a dressing room, slipping on the highest
heels she'd ever seen in her life. With her new dress and
shoes on, she took a deep breath and walked out to look
in the mirror.

It felt like every head in the store turned. Barbara's form-fitting black dress revealed a banging figure and a strangely comfortable posture. Not only that, her hair looked amazing. It was wild and perfectly curly. Her makeup was on point too. Barbara looked in the mirror, almost not recognizing herself. She'd never dressed like this before—her usual look was a lot more retiring, a lot more modest. But Barbara wasn't feeling modest. She was feeling confident . . . she was feeling strong . . . she was feeling pretty.

Later that night, as Barbara strode up the steps to the museum gala in her fabulous outfit, she was finally able to pinpoint it. *Huh,* she thought. *I think I actually kind of feel like how I'm sure Diana feels.*

"Dr. Minerva?" a voice said behind her. Barbara twirled neatly on her heels to see—

"Maxwell!" she breathed. Maxwell Lord smiled at her, and she melted a little. He looked so handsome—he was wearing a broad-shouldered inky-black tuxedo that was nipped in at the waist for a perfect silhouette. His dark eyes shone in the thousand twinkling lights of the gala.

"You look . . . breathtaking," he said, stammering a little. Barbara blushed. To think she could make a man like Maxwell Lord nervous!

"Oh, *this* old thing?" Barbara said. She twirled a little, showing it off. "I've worn it to *so* many parties—I go to parties like this all the time, you know."

Then she hesitated. It didn't really feel like *her* talking. And she didn't like that. She took a deep breath.

"That's not really true," Barbara admitted sheepishly. She looked down and fiddled with the hem of her short dress. "I don't usually look so good. Or fit in so well. Or fit in . . . at all. Actually."

Maxwell hesitated a moment, catching Barbara's eyes. Then he said, "Me either."

Barbara could hardly believe it. Maxwell felt like an outsider too? But he was so charming, so confident, so rich. *I guess everyone has their secrets,* Barbara thought. Even Maxwell. Maybe especially Maxwell. She just couldn't believe he'd trust her with that. She couldn't believe he was being so vulnerable with her.

Then the shy, vulnerable look on Maxwell's face faded and was replaced with the cocky, charming grin that she'd already gotten to know so well. "It's so loud in here!" Maxwell said. "Want to go somewhere where we can really talk?"

"Sure!" Barbara said.

"Your office?" Maxwell suggested.

Barbara shrugged. She didn't really care *where* they went, as long as she could be with Maxwell.

When they got to Barbara's office, Maxwell seemed weirdly fascinated by the stuff Barbara kept there. She remembered, suddenly, how he'd barged in that morning, looking at her desk with such interest. It was odd. But Barbara pushed the thought out of her head.

"Look at all of this," Maxwell said, throwing his arms wide and turning so his gesture took in Barbara's entire office. He looked enchanted. Barbara looked around. Her office didn't seem so special to her. There were a few chairs, her desk, a messy pile of files, a poster from Italy on her wall (she'd never been, but *oh*, how she wanted to go), and a few random bits of exhibits and artifacts that she was working on—including that silly citrine whatever-it-was that the FBI had brought in for identification.

"It's all so beautiful," Maxwell said grandiosely. He swept Barbara into his arms. "Just like you," he murmured, and she blushed scarlet.

"Th-thanks," she stammered.

Maxwell let go with one hand and picked something up off her desk. "Just like *this*," he said, holding up the citrine between them. He turned it around for a moment in his fingers, letting the light catch it. His other arm was still wrapped around Barbara's waist. It was making it hard for her to think. She wished Maxwell would stop looking at the citrine and look at *her* again.

"What *is* this, anyway?" Maxwell asked casually.

"Uh," Barbara said blankly. "It's nothing special. Just something I'm trying to identify for the FBI. But I'm pretty stumped so far."

Maxwell looked excited. "Let me help!" he said. "I have a dear friend who's an expert in Roman antiquities who could take a look."

Barbara squinted at him, confused. Was what it with him and this rock? But Maxwell misunderstood her look. "That *is* Latin, isn't it?" he asked, gesturing at the writing engraved on the gold setting of the gem.

"Yes," Barbara said reluctantly. Maybe letting Maxwell take the stone to his friend would make him happy. Maybe it would make him like her more. But she really wasn't supposed to let other people walk off with artifacts from the museum. She could lose her job!

That's a dumb rule anyway, Barbara thought rebelliously. Maxwell wanted the stone, and Maxwell was wonderful. It would be mean to stop him. And plus,

he was going to be a special friend of the museum part-
ners or something, which meant that he was probably
entitled to take whatever he wanted anyway.

Maxwell clutched the stone and smiled.

"Steve," Diana whispered. Her throat closed and she
nearly choked on the word. How was this possible? Was
it real?

"Diana," he murmured back, reaching out and trac-
ing his fingertips down the side of her face. "It really is
you," he said. "I can't believe it."

Tears swam in Diana's eyes. She'd dreamed about
this for decades. She'd heard Steve's voice echoing in
her head almost every day for over sixty years. But she'd
never imagined she would ever see him again.

He had been dead, and gone.

And now—somehow—he wasn't.

"How . . . ," Diana started. She swallowed, choking
her tears back. "How are you . . ."

"I have absolutely no idea," Steve said. He smiled
helplessly, and there they were—those sweet laugh lines

at the corners of his eyes. Suddenly the joy of his return hit Diana all at once.

She threw her arms around him, laughing, burying her smile in his shoulder, as he wrapped his arms around her and held her tight.

Diana and Steve escaped the gala as quickly as they could and found refuge in the quiet night, strolling along the reflecting pool in the heart of DC. Diana couldn't quite talk herself into letting go of Steve's hand, but he didn't seem to mind—he clutched hers tightly in his.

"What do you remember?" Diana asked him after they'd walked in silence for a while.

"I remember . . . ," Steve started, frowning thoughtfully. "I remember the airfield. Flying the plane up. And then . . . nothing, really. But somehow I know I've also been somewhere else since then. Somewhere I can't put words to."

He paused. His face was solemn but not unhappy. "But it's good, that other place," he said. "It's good."

Diana nodded and felt something unclench deep in her heart. Steve hadn't been suffering. Then she looked up, searching his face.

"It worked, you know," she told him. "What you did with the plane. You saved us."

Steve smiled. "Good," he said.

They walked a bit farther in companionable silence.

"So anyway," Steve said after a while, "I woke up here."

"Where exactly?" Diana asked.

"In a bed," Steve said, frowning. "But a strange bed. It was like a giant pillow. On slats?"

Diana nodded. "A futon," she said. Steve wouldn't be familiar with futons—they had only made it to the US from Japan recently.

"Say," Steve said, "I know a lot of time has passed. But what year is it exactly?"

"It's 1984," Diana said.

"Wow," Steve said in a hushed voice. A massive jet flew over them in the night sky on its way to Washington National Airport. Steve followed it with his gaze, craning his neck.

"Amazing," he murmured. Then he looked down at Diana, the moonlight glinting in his eyes. "But not as amazing as this right here," he added. Diana grinned helplessly. She couldn't remember feeling this happy—ever.

The two reunited lovers walked arm in arm for a long time in the warm, quiet DC night.

Barbara wandered home in a daze. Had she ever felt this happy? She'd had such a lovely evening with Maxwell. She sighed dreamily. He was such a gentleman. So handsome. So smart! And he really liked her!

But then—what wasn't to like? Barbara looked down at herself as she walked home. She was dressed to the nines and pulling it off effortlessly. Her makeup hadn't gotten smudged all night. Her hair had been perfect too—not a single hair-sprayed lock had dared stray out of place. Something had changed. But what?

You made a wish, she thought.

But that was silly. That rock was a fake. An ancient fake, maybe, but a fake. There was nothing special about it, and it's not like wishes really *could* be granted in the first place.

Barbara stuffed the whole thing out of her mind. She was finally home, and it was time for bed. She pulled her new crystal-embellished stilettos off at the door to her apartment and chucked them in the direction of the coat closet. Spot was sleeping with his fluffy belly up on her bed.

But her brain was buzzing. She felt too good to sleep!

I've always wanted to learn Italian, she thought out of nowhere. *Why not tonight?*

Or she could finally finish sewing those new covers for her couch cushions. Or she could finally read that book about early nineteenth-century archeological practices as pertaining to gemology. Or—

This place is a mess, she thought. *That's the first thing.* She turned and went to the little pantry closet next to the kitchen, where she kept cleaning supplies. She'd tackle that first. And then, after her apartment was clean, she'd move on from there.

Six hours later, dawn broke over Washington, DC, and Barbara was ready for it. She was spotlessly dressed in her best work outfit, her kitchen and bathroom were gleaming, she'd repainted the living-room walls, cleaned the gutters outside her apartment, made herself a gourmet breakfast, and read a couple of books.

Sleep? Who needed it?

Not Barbara Minerva!

SIX

Maxwell Lord's car screeched to a halt halfway onto the sidewalk in front of the darkened facade of the Black Gold Cooperative offices. It was late, late at night, and there was nobody around.

Not that there was anybody here during the day, either, Maxwell thought sourly as he let himself into the lobby and hurried across the cold marble floor, his footsteps echoing in the darkness. Black Gold Cooperative was a bust, an empty shell, a nothingness.

But that was about to change. Because *Maxwell* was about to change.

Maxwell nearly ran across the cavernous office space, dodging the unused phones that lay sadly on big, empty tables where workstations had once been planned.

Finally he got to his office and flicked on the light. He shut the door behind him, taking the time to lock it. Yes, it was the wee hours of the night. But Maxwell still wasn't taking any chances. He needed to be uninterrupted.

Maxwell swept his desk clear. Years' worth of clippings, Xeroxes, and manuscripts went flying and fluttering to the floor. Most of them were about the same thing—the subject of Maxwell's obsessive research for the last decade. An ancient rumor. A myth that most people said was just that—mythological. Not real. Impossible, imaginary.

A Dreamstone.

Maxwell snorted. Nearly everyone who had studied it said it didn't exist. The few who admitted that it might be real said it would never be found.

But he had found it. Or rather, the FBI had stumbled across it without realizing what they'd found. They'd sent it to the Smithsonian, and Maxwell's whisper network had brought him word of it. And then sweet, pretty Barbara Minerva had been so happy to let him into her office, where it had been sitting on her desk as though it was another paperweight.

Maxwell paused at the thought of Barbara. He had been using her, yes. But there was something about her. A strange combination of confidence and vulnerability, of beauty and awkwardness. She didn't fit in, but she was trying. Maxwell could relate. He *did* relate.

I hope I see her again, Maxwell thought. And then he put Barbara Minerva out of his mind. He had something more important to think about now. He'd found the Dreamstone. Maxwell had spent his whole life trying to please people, trying to build a business empire around being everything to everyone. Making peoples' dreams come true, all the way to the bank.

Now nothing could stop him. Not if this worked.

It had to work. It *had* to.

With shaking hands, Maxwell laid the stone down on his bare desk.

"One great wish," he murmured, his eyes skimming over the now-familiar Latin inscription around the gold setting.

He put one hand over the stone.

"I wish for your power," Maxwell told it.

A cold breeze ruffled his hair. But that was it.

Nothing had happened. Maxwell felt his heart sinking. Was this it? Had he reached his last, greatest hope, only to be disappointed? The debtors were at his door. The feds were going to start sniffing around soon. Black Gold Cooperative was about to go belly-up, and it might well land Maxwell in jail. His only chance had been the

Dreamstone. Was it really—

And then Maxwell's whole body spasmed as raw power arced through him. Before his eyes were forced shut by the supernatural forces that were lighting up his bones, he saw a gale wind tear through the office.

Then everything went white-hot.

Maxwell came back to himself in pieces. First he remembered his office—papers everywhere, a bookcase fallen across his desk. Then a flash of the early dawn on the DC streets as he staggered out of Black Gold Cooperative. His hands on the steering wheel of his car. A stoplight. A phone booth.

But it wasn't until he was tying a richly worked silk tie around his neck and giving his still-damp hair one last tidy comb that Maxwell fully woke up. He put the comb down on the vanity counter and stared at himself in the mirror. He was wearing his best suit. He was freshly shaved and smelled faintly of expensive cologne. Automatically, his hand reached for a tiepin, and he watched himself place it perfectly in the center of his tie.

Maxwell looked like a million bucks. But that was nothing new—he usually looked like a million bucks. It was his job.

But he felt . . . he felt different. Except that saying he felt different was like saying that an apple was different from the planet Jupiter.

Maxwell was *changed*. There was something inside him that was bigger than he was—bigger than the whole world. A power that was barely restraining itself from bleeding out of his eyes, his ears, the edges of his fingernails.

"I did it," Maxwell murmured.

And he knew what he was going to do next. He'd been planning for this for a very long time.

Forty minutes later, Maxwell Lord's car glided to a stop in front of a slick glass office tower. Etched into the facade were the words STAGG INDUSTRIES.

Maxwell Lord strode right by the security desk and swanned into Simon Stagg's office.

Stagg stood up from his desk. He looked Maxwell up and down with an unfriendly sneer. "You better be here with my money," he said.

Maxwell waved a hand dismissively. "I'll have your money, Simon," he said. "But today, I'm here for an apology."

Stagg's face turned an alarming shade of red. "You must be out of your damn—" he started. But Maxwell cut him off.

"*I'm sorry,*" he told Stagg. "That's the apology—it's mine. I'm sorry, Simon. I messed up."

Stagg was so surprised by this that he plopped right back down into his chair. Maxwell went on. "The truth is, I knew we were going to sink a long time ago. The wells, which you paid for, were coming up dry. And no data suggested that was going to change. I should have folded right then."

Maxwell sighed dramatically. "But there were all the people that had bought in," he continued, "that believed in me. People like you, Simon. I wanted to be right. I wanted so badly to be able to take care of *you*, for once. To finally come to you with good news."

Maxwell let his eyes tear up a bit for effect. He knew he was being sort of a ham, but he could see that Stagg was completely taken in.

Stagg looked uncomfortable. "Maxwell, come on," he said. "You don't have to—"

Maxwell interrupted him again. "Don't you think I wished for better?" he asked. He put a bit of emphasis on "wish."

"With every ounce of my being," he continued, "I wished that Black Gold would change the world for all of us. I wished that it would exceed everyone's wildest hopes and dreams."

Maxwell was staring intently into Stagg's eyes. Stagg stared back, captivated. Maxwell leaned in and put his hand on Stagg's arm.

"I know that you wish for that too," Maxwell said. He locked eyes with Stagg. "Don't you."

Say it, Maxwell thought. *Say it, damn you. I need you to say it.*

"Of course I wish that," Stagg said, looking perplexed. "But—"

But the wish had been made. Maxwell had everything he needed. He straightened up and adjusted his tie, all the intensity draining out of him in a moment.

"Your wish is granted," Maxwell said breezily. He grinned at Stagg and strolled out of his office.

One down.

"These cars are so fast!" Steve said, staring at the traffic going by on the DC streets. He was walking Diana to her office, but her usual morning route was taking four times as long because there was so much for Steve to take in. Not that Diana minded—any time spent with Steve was time well spent. And she loved watching him marvel at the technological advances that marked the modern world.

This morning, while trying to get dressed, he questioned why he was putting on pants called parachute pants and if people parachuted everywhere now. Diana remembered laughing; he was like a kid on Christmas morning. Sweet and endearing. Steve had hopped straight from 1918 to 1984—Diana could hardly imagine how jarring that must be to experience. She remembered when she had first come to this world. The first time she'd tasted ice cream. The first time she had tried on a dress. It was the first time she felt different from everyone else. Out of place. Out of time. She remembered how frightening and disorienting that felt.

But Steve didn't seem frightened or disoriented—he seemed delighted. And that delighted Diana.

Diana steered Steve into a subway station, and they found themselves at the top of an unusually long escalator down to the subway platform. Steve stopped dead, staring down at the moving staircase. "Yikes," he murmured.

Diana laughed at the look of trepidation on his face.

Steve laughed a little too, and stepped carefully onto the escalator. "Fine," he said, rolling his eyes at her. "Laugh at the old guy."

The subway platform itself offered more strange sights for Steve. Diana was used to the odd habits and fashions of mankind in 1984, but she enjoyed seeing it all freshly through Steve's eyes. Punk rockers with multicolored Mohawk hairdos sulked at the edges of the platform. Break dancers spun to hip-hop beats on mats made of broken-down cardboard boxes, holding their baseball hats out to collect change from the small crowd watching them. A self-important businessman talked loudly on an expensive mobile phone as he waited for the subway train.

Diana watched Steve take it all in, fascinated, delighted, and she found herself fascinated and delighted too. *I live here,* Diana thought. *I commute this way every morning. So why do I feel like I'm seeing all this for the first time?* Had she been that disconnected? That distant? How strange, that having Steve back would help anchor her to this time, to this place. It was fitting, she supposed—perhaps missing him had been part of what had held Diana apart from the world.

The subway train arrived, and Diana and Steve found their seats.

"So," Steve said, picking up a conversation they'd started earlier, "a stone did this?" He gestured at himself.

Diana frowned thoughtfully. "That's what we have to go and find out. It must have done *something*."

The citrine fake had been on Diana's mind all night. It was just too much of a coincidence. First she'd made a sad, hopeless wish on a fake talisman, and then, the very next day, she discovered that her wish had come true.

She hoped Barbara would still have the stone in her office and would be willing to let Diana take another look. Diana smiled, remembering how desolate she'd felt when Barbara had asked her if she'd ever been in love. All she'd been able to think was, *Yes, once, and never again*. But now here she was, with the only man she'd ever loved, watching him discover a new universe of bad smells on the DC subway.

The subway doors opened. "This is us," Diana said, and led Steve off the train.

"Thank goodness," he murmured.

Back aboveground, Diana and Steve found themselves walking past the National Air and Space Museum. A huge banner hung in front of it, with a photo of the space shuttle. Steve stopped in his tracks when he saw it.

"Is that a plane?" he said uncertainly.

Diana grinned. Of course! Steve had been gone for the entire age of human spaceflight. He had *no idea*. And Diana didn't know anyone who loved flying as much as Steve did—or flying machines.

"Come on," she said. She'd be late to work—but who cared? She was a millennia-old demigod crime fighter whose human boyfriend had been miraculously revived from the dead. She could afford the slap on the wrist. And Steve was going to lose his mind when he saw the Apollo 11.

Diana and Steve took their time with the air and space museum. Steve hardly spoke as they moved through the huge spaces, taking in the space shuttle, the Apollo 11 moon lander, stage-one rockets from nearly every NASA project. . . .

After a while spent wandering the museum, Steve turned to Diana, wonder written all over his face. "They put a man in space," he said. His voice was nearly a whisper.

"A woman too," Diana pointed out.

Steve smiled. "It's incredible," he said. "And I missed it. But you didn't. What was it like?"

Diana was taken aback. He was asking her?

"I—I don't know," she admitted. "I didn't watch it."

Steve shook his head, shocked. "What? Why not?" he asked.

Diana struggled to find words to make him understand. "It's . . . I'm not of their world," she said finally. "This isn't my home. Not really. So sometimes I try to just—I keep my distance."

Steve looked at her uncomprehendingly.

"It's safer that way," Diana finished. Her voice sounded small to her own ears. Small, and cowardly.

SEVEN

Maxwell stared out the window of his car as it oozed through the morning rush-hour DC traffic. He'd felt something when he told Stagg that his wish was granted. Maxwell was sure of it. *Something* had happened—something that had to do with this roiling ball of weird power that was beating at his fingertips and the backs of his eyeballs. But what? Had he really granted Stagg's wish? Was Black Gold Cooperative finally going to succeed now?

Or would the wish be gradual? Maybe he'd arrive at the office and the first hesitant buyers would just be arriving, wondering why they'd decided to do this, *today*.

But when Maxwell's car pulled up in front of Black Gold Cooperative, nothing had changed.

Maxwell's hope turned bitter in his mouth as he got out of the car and walked, defeated, into the building. The lobby was empty. Not even Raquel, his long-suffering secretary and only actual employee, was there.

Maybe she decided enough was enough, Maxwell thought bitterly. The phone at her desk was ringing and ringing with nobody to answer it.

But it wasn't just that phone. As Maxwell made his way across the lobby toward the frosted glass doors leading to the office space of Black Gold, he heard them:

Hundreds of phones, all ringing.

Maxwell's heart lurched. He burst through the doors to find Raquel hurrying from phone to phone, desperately trying to take orders and keep customers on the line as more and more people called.

"What happened?" Maxwell asked. But he knew the answer.

"The wells," Raquel said. She straightened up and stared at him like the world's happiest deer in the headlights. "They struck pay."

"Which ones?" Maxwell asked.

Raquel shook her head. "Texas," she said. "Mississippi. *All* of them." She dodged off to answer a few more calls. "Please hold," she said, hitting a button on one phone and then running to the next. "Black Gold Cooperative, please hold."

She returned to Maxwell, looking even more harried. "Somehow all of the investors heard about it. They're calling to up their buys. Their friends are calling to buy in. New investors are calling out of thin air. Mr. Lord, *I need more help.*"

Maxwell thought fast. He stepped toward Raquel and took her by the shoulders, making sure his grip was firm. "I'll get you help," he said reassuringly. "Tell me again—you *wish* you had more help?"

Raquel shook her head impatiently. "Yes, I wish I had more help!" she cried. "There's just too many—"

Knock, knock.

Maxwell and Raquel spun around. A young man in a smart pinstripe suit stood in the doorway from the lobby.

"Hi," he said sheepishly. He waved a folder in his hand. "I'm sorry to bother you. I was interviewing at the accounting firm next door, but—"

"You're hired," Maxwell said.

"Yes!" the kid said, pumping his fist in the air.

"Welcome aboard . . . ," Maxwell started.

"Emerson." The kid filled in his name for Maxwell.

Another man popped his head in the door. "Hi," he said. "I was wondering if you're—"

"Yep. You're hired too," Maxwell said. Raquel heaved a sigh of relief and stuffed a telephone into Emerson's hand.

It was working.

I did it, Maxwell thought. *This is it. I did it. It's done.*

He was going to be rich. Rich beyond his wildest dreams. Everything from here would be smooth sailing.

Raquel hurried up again, bringing one of the phones with her, its cord stretching as far as she could pull it. "It's the *Wall Street Journal,*" she hissed. "They want to interview you about the company's sudden surge."

Maxwell smiled. The tension of the last year of failure was finally seeping out of him. "I'll take it in my office," he said. He took the phone and swaggered into his office with it. This was going to be *fun.*

Barbara stretched as she woke up from what had to be the best night's sleep of her life. Feeling energized, she headed to the kitchen to make herself some breakfast. She reached for the refrigerator door when—

SHABANG!

The door ripped from the hinges and was now being held up by only her hand.

What the . . . ? she thought. *This hunk of junk must've just been on its last leg.*

Barbara knew it had been an accident, but the fridge incident that morning had made her feel strangely powerful. She had a little time to kill before she needed to leave for work, so she decided to stop by the gym in her apartment building.

When she arrived at the gym, Barbara looked around. She'd come down here with the idea of picking up some weights, but now that she was looking around at the rowing machine, the treadmills, and the various weight-training rigs, she really kind of wanted to try everything.

Well, why not?

She started with the free weights. She was able to lift a pretty hefty barbell without much trouble, so she moved on to a stacked bar. Squaring her feet under her, she reached down and heaved the weight up to her shoulders, then over her head, then back down again. Easy. Barbara glanced at the weighted disks that had been loaded onto the bar and did a bit of quick math in her head.

Three hundred pounds.

She tilted her head. *Huh.*

Then she shrugged, ignoring the surprised gym goers, and moved on to the treadmill. Barbara mashed her finger down on the "faster" button and started running, and running—until she was moving at a full sprint.

"Faster!" Barbara told the machine, jabbing the arrow button with her finger again and again. Her feet flew below her as she raced to match the treadmill. It was too easy. She wanted to go faster! Did this lousy machine really top out at twenty miles per hour?

She jabbed the button again, and something behind the console gave a hissing, spitting noise. The machine groaned to a halt and started to smoke gently. Barbara leaped off the treadmill and caught a glimpse of herself in the wall-to-wall mirror of the gym. Her eyes were gleaming and she was holding herself like—

Like she wanted to pounce. Barbara had a glint in her eyes and a smirk on her face. She was enjoying this.

She grabbed her purse and headed to work. She hadn't even broken a sweat.

Work was way more fun now that Barbara was . . . well, now that *she* was way more fun too. She'd arrived at the office more or less on time and had gotten maybe ten minutes of actual work done before she'd gotten bored and waltzed into the lab to see what her coworkers were getting up to. Within minutes, she was perched on a table in the lab space, holding court. Barbara's colleagues were crowded around her, hanging on her every word.

"You're right, Roger," Barbara said, waving the jade Chinese lion in his direction. It was number nineteen from the FBI's collection of artifacts that Barbara had been examining. "I actually read a few books about this last night, and it *is* from the Song dynasty."

Roger high-fived Jake.

"But!" Barbara added, wagging a perfectly manicured finger at him, "Lucy was correct about its striation. And—"

Barbara paused to check her notes. She squinted through her glasses at her notebook. It was hopelessly blurry. She took her glasses off, and the writing sprang into focus with no trouble.

"Weird," Barbara said. "All of this midnight reading has apparently *cured* my eyesight."

The door opened. Barbara tossed her glasses aside and smiled to see Diana walk in. And—what was this? A handsome guy was walking with her.

"This is Steve," Diana said, gesturing at the guy. "He's . . ." She trailed off, looking a little lost.

"I'm an old friend of Diana's," Steve finished for her. "Nice to meet you."

Many years later, Diana was living among mortals. The year was 1984, and everything was different. Focused on saving the innocent, Diana's deeds were getting attention.

"POLICE AND BYSTANDERS ARE REPORTING THAT THE ROBBERY WAS FOILED BY A MYSTERIOUS FEMALE SAVIOR."

DIANA HAD BECOME KNOWN AS *Wonder Woman!*

Barbara shook his hand. *I thought Diana said she didn't* have *any old friends,* she thought. *But I'm happy to be wrong. Diana deserves some nice people in her life.*

"Hello, old friend," Barbara said out loud. She winked at Steve. "I'm Diana's *new* friend, Barbara."

"Pleasure," Steve said, ducking his head sweetly.

"So what do you do, Steve?" Barbara asked. She was dying to know more about this guy. Diana really was a mystery wrapped in an enigma. Where'd she been keeping this cutie?

"I'm a pilot," Steve said.

Barbara's mind went blank for a moment. A pilot? Hadn't Diana said . . . when Barbara had asked her if she'd ever been in love—

But she'd said he'd *died.*

Barbara shook her head. This couldn't be the same guy Diana had been talking about at dinner. That guy was dead. Diana had said so.

"Can I talk to you for a second?" Diana asked.

Barbara nodded. "Sure," she said. "Of course."

They headed back to Barbara's office, and Steve tagged along, sticking close to Diana. *Something weird is going on with this dude,* Barbara thought. But she couldn't quite put her finger on it.

Diana closed the door to Barbara's office behind them.

"I wanted to ask you about that stone," she said. "The citrine one. Do you have it?"

Barbara winced. She had really hoped this wouldn't come up.

"Oh, yeah," she said casually. "It's a long story. Maxwell came by, and I—well, I let him borrow it."

"You let him *borrow* it?" Diana said, her entire body stiffening.

Barbara shrank back a bit.

"He just gave the museum a *huge* amount of money, Diana!" she said defensively. "It's not like he's a stranger. *And* he has a friend who's an expert. He's going to help us ID the thing. It's a favor to—"

"How could you *lend* it to—" Diana interrupted her, but Barbara tore right back in.

"Why do you even *care*?" she asked, narrowing her eyes. "There are probably fifty items in this office that are more valuable and more interesting than that phony rock. Like my stapler, for example. What's the big deal, anyway?"

"Barbara," Diana said in a steady voice, "I'm sorry. But I need to see that stone."

"What is it?" Barbara asked.

Once a year, the Amazons all gathered together in the huge sta[dium] for the Amazon Games. Diana, the young princess of the Amazons, competed, but she lost. Diana's mother comforted her when victory was ripped away from her.

"ONE DAY YOU'LL BECOME ALL THE THINGS YOU DREAM OF AND MORE. AND THEN EVERYTHING WILL BE DIFFERENT."

A NEW FRIEND

When she wasn't fighting crime as Wonder Woman, Diana worked at the Smithsonian Museum. One day she met Dr. Barbara Minerva. Barbara was working on identifying a mysterious stone.

Diana took Barbara to lunch and noticed that Barbara lacked self-confidence. Barbara sometimes wished she could be more like Diana.

Meanwhile, a businessman named Maxwell Lord was running a corrupt corporation that sold oil stock to unsuspecting customers.

"WELCOME TO BLACK GOLD COOPERATIVE! THE WORLD'S FIRST OIL COMPANY RUN FOR THE PEOPLE, BY THE PEOPLE. YOU CAN OWN A PIECE OF THE MOST LUCRATIVE INDUSTRY IN THE WORLD. AND EVERY TIME WE STRIKE GOLD, YOU STRIKE GOLD."

Maxwell Lord wanted only one thing: total power.

Diana wanted something as well. She wanted the love of her life, Steve Trevor, to come back. His plane had been destroyed over forty years ago. Then one day, Diana's dream came true.

DIANA AND STEVE WERE FINALLY REUNITED.

Not only did Diana get what she wanted, but so did Barbara. She felt a sudden change and became more and more confident. She began to take on powerful abilities, and with them, Barbara became more and more power hungry.

"IT TURNS OUT THAT WISHING 'TO BE LIKE DIANA' CAME WITH SOME SURPRISES."

BARBARA BECAME *The Cheetah*

With the world in grave danger, Diana knew she would need all of her strength and powers. She finally donned the golden armor—a lost treasure of the Amazons.

SHE HAD A WORLD TO SAVE.

"I'll let you know when I do," Diana said. She nodded at Steve. "Let's go."

Although concerned, Diana watched and couldn't help but be amused and happy as Steve practically hung out of the window of the cab that was speeding them toward Black Gold's offices.

"The pickup on this thing!" Steve said, ducking his head back in to grin at Diana, his wind-tousled hair falling over his eyes. "It's incredible, Diana!"

Diana smiled and brushed his bangs back out of his eyes. Steve's grin quieted to something more thoughtful—something just for her. He caught her hand and kissed the backs of her fingers, like a knight from one of those fairy tales people liked to tell each other.

"Sorry, but I can't get any closer," the cab driver said, and Diana tore her gaze away from Steve's perfectly blue eyes to look outside. They'd arrived at the Black Gold offices, but the cab had slowed to a halt about a hundred feet from the front door. The building was absolutely mobbed—news vans, police cars, civilian cars, and at least five hundred people on foot were all jammed in around the building. It was utter chaos. People were banging on the doors of the office building, banging on the windows. Many of them were waving fistfuls of cash, or clutching checkbooks.

Diana and Steve leaped out of the cab and took in the scene.

"What are these people *doing*?" Steve wondered aloud.

"Take our calls!" someone in the crowd started yelling. "Take our calls!" Other people took up the cry, and soon the crowd was roaring in unison. A man climbed halfway up a telephone pole and yelled, "Provide equal opportunity to invest!"

Diana looked at Steve and shrugged helplessly. She had no idea what was going on.

"Whatever it is," she yelled, raising her voice so Steve could hear her over the crowd, "we need to find another way in!"

Steve looked around, craning his neck and scanning the area. Then he grabbed Diana's hand. "Come on," he said, leading her through the crowd toward the side of the building.

They looped around the edge of the Black Gold building and found a quiet loading area on the opposite side of the block.

Barbara shook his hand. *I thought Diana said she didn't have any old friends,* she thought. *But I'm happy to be wrong. Diana deserves some nice people in her life.*

"Hello, old friend," Barbara said out loud. She winked at Steve. "I'm Diana's *new* friend, Barbara."

"Pleasure," Steve said, ducking his head sweetly.

"So what do you do, Steve?" Barbara asked. She was dying to know more about this guy. Diana really was a mystery wrapped in an enigma. Where'd she been keeping this cutie?

"I'm a pilot," Steve said.

Barbara's mind went blank for a moment. A pilot? Hadn't Diana said . . . when Barbara had asked her if she'd ever been in love—

But she'd said he'd *died.*

Barbara shook her head. This couldn't be the same guy Diana had been talking about at dinner. That guy was dead. Diana had said so.

"Can I talk to you for a second?" Diana asked.

Barbara nodded. "Sure," she said. "Of course."

They headed back to Barbara's office, and Steve tagged along, sticking close to Diana. *Something weird is going on with this dude,* Barbara thought. But she couldn't quite put her finger on it.

Diana closed the door to Barbara's office behind them.

"I wanted to ask you about that stone," she said. "The citrine one. Do you have it?"

Barbara winced. She had really hoped this wouldn't come up.

"Oh, yeah," she said casually. "It's a long story. Maxwell came by, and I—well, I let him borrow it."

"You let him *borrow* it?" Diana said, her entire body stiffening.

Barbara shrank back a bit.

"He just gave the museum a *huge* amount of money, Diana!" she said defensively. "It's not like he's a stranger. *And* he has a friend who's an expert. He's going to help us ID the thing. It's a favor to—"

"How could you *lend* it to—" Diana interrupted her, but Barbara tore right back in.

"Why do you even *care*?" she asked, narrowing her eyes. "There are probably fifty items in this office that are more valuable and more interesting than that phony rock. Like my stapler, for example. What's the big deal, anyway?"

"Barbara," Diana said in a steady voice, "I'm sorry. But I need to see that stone."

"What is it?" Barbara asked.

Once a year, the Amazons all gathered together in the huge stadium for the Amazon Games. Diana, the young princess of the Amazons, competed, but she lost. Diana's mother comforted her when victory was ripped away from her.

"ONE DAY YOU'LL BECOME ALL THE THINGS YOU DREAM OF AND MORE. AND THEN EVERYTHING WILL BE DIFFERENT."

Many years later, Diana was living among mortals. The year was 1984, and everything was different. Focused on saving the innocent, Diana's deeds were getting attention.

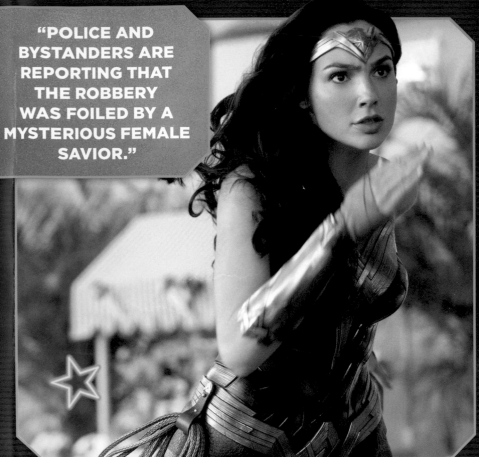

"POLICE AND BYSTANDERS ARE REPORTING THAT THE ROBBERY WAS FOILED BY A MYSTERIOUS FEMALE SAVIOR."

DIANA HAD BECOME KNOWN AS

Wonder Woman!

Not only did Diana get what she wanted, but so did Barbara. She felt a sudden change and became more and more confident. She began to take on powerful abilities, and with them, Barbara became more and more power hungry.

"IT TURNS OUT THAT WISHING 'TO BE LIKE DIANA' CAME WITH SOME SURPRISES."

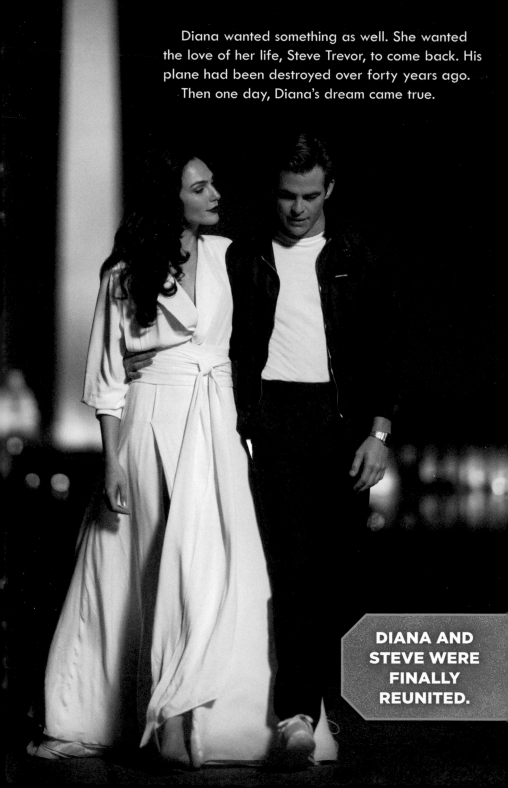

Diana wanted something as well. She wanted the love of her life, Steve Trevor, to come back. His plane had been destroyed over forty years ago. Then one day, Diana's dream came true.

DIANA AND STEVE WERE FINALLY REUNITED.

Meanwhile, a businessman named Maxwell Lord was running a corrupt corporation that sold oil stock to unsuspecting customers.

"WELCOME TO BLACK GOLD COOPERATIVE! THE WORLD'S FIRST OIL COMPANY RUN FOR THE PEOPLE, BY THE PEOPLE. YOU CAN OWN A PIECE OF THE MOST LUCRATIVE INDUSTRY IN THE WORLD. AND EVERY TIME WE STRIKE GOLD, YOU STRIKE GOLD."

Maxwell Lord wanted only one thing: total power.

A NEW FRIEND

When she wasn't fighting crime as Wonder Woman, Diana worked at the Smithsonian Museum. One day she met Dr. Barbara Minerva. Barbara was working on identifying a mysterious stone.

Diana took Barbara to lunch and noticed that Barbara lacked self-confidence. Barbara sometimes wished she could be more like Diana.

"This must be the other side of the building," Steve said, looking up at the featureless brick wall. It had one garage door with a padlock on it.

Steve tried the door. It was locked—firmly.

He stepped back, looked at Diana with a raised eyebrow, and made an elaborate "Be my guest" kind of gesture at the door. Diana grinned and ripped it open.

Diana and Steve hurried into the building. They were in a service hallway, which was dark and quiet, but even there they could hear the din of phones ringing and voices chattering in excitement. "This way," Diana said, hurrying up some stairs toward the noise.

They burst onto the trading floor and stopped in shock. Workmen were unloading office furniture from huge wooden pallets. In some cases they were assembling cubicles around workers who were already on the phones, racing from one call to the next, frantically jotting down orders and passing them off to runners who were scurrying to and fro. Electricians wove their way through the fray, wiring new phones and new lights into the space.

Something very strange was happening here, and Diana had a bad feeling she knew what it was.

"Come on," Diana said, jerking her head toward the back of the space. She'd spotted Maxwell Lord's office.

Diana and Steve made their way through the chaos of the Black Gold Cooperative sales floor completely unnoticed. Everybody was too busy to look up. They slipped into Maxwell Lord's empty office and closed the door softly behind them.

Diana looked around Lord's office. She'd been expecting a mess—Lord seemed like the kind of man who would have a messy office—but this was beyond a mess. The room looked like it had been hit by a tornado. Drifts of loose papers were strewn around, piled up in corners and around the large carved-wood desk.

Steve was poking around, looking for the citrine. Diana joined him, sifting through the fallen papers, the books, the random knickknacks. But the stone was nowhere to be found. The books and papers were almost as interesting as the stone, however. Many of them were about ancient artifacts. Others were about dreams and wishes. And Steve held up a clipping of a news story detailing how a shipment of stolen artifacts had been recovered by the FBI and sent to the Smithsonian for identification.

"Whatever that stone is," Steve said, "he's been looking for it for a long time. There are research journals here that date back years."

Diana frowned and nodded. Maxwell Lord had known that there was something special about that stone, and he'd been hunting it. Why? She looked around again, hoping she'd missed something—and she had.

Something glinted from under a sheaf of dot-matrix printouts. Diana moved the pages aside and picked it up. It was the gold fitting from the citrine. It was bent and gnarled—and the stone that it had encircled was gone. But Diana remembered it. She turned it around in her fingers, examining it. There was the inscription she'd seen before: *On This Object Held, Cast but One Great Wish,* it said in carefully engraved Latin.

But there were words on the gold ring that she hadn't seen before, because they'd been engraved into the inside surface—the surface that had been pressed against the stone itself. And these words were not in Latin.

Diana's blood ran cold. She dropped the metal ring like it was on fire, and it clattered onto Maxwell Lord's desk.

Steve crossed the room in two big strides. "What is it?" he asked, staring down at the ring.

"The interior," Diana whispered. "It has an inscription written in the language of the gods."

Steve stared at her, his eyes wide.

"But which god wrote it?" Diana continued, her voice still hoarse. She felt her hands shaking and clenched them together to make them stop. "That is the question we need to figure out."

Diana had a complicated history with gods. She knew just how destructive they could be.

She reached for the phone on Maxwell Lord's desk and swept her finger around the rotary dial, calling a number she knew by heart: the museum.

Soon she'd been patched through to Barbara.

"Barbara!" Diana said before Barbara could even say hello. "I need your help."

"Uh—" Barbara started, but Diana cut her off again.

"Find out everything you can about *where* that citrine was found, okay?" She locked eyes with Steve as she spoke into the phone. "*Where* is what I need to know," she said.

"Got it," Barbara said crisply. "I'm on it."

Diana set the headset down in the cradle of the phone and sighed.

"You look like you saw a ghost," Steve said, taking her gently by the arm.

"I sort of did," Diana answered. "In a way."

Steve cocked his head. "You see," Diana went on, "there were *many* gods once. And they did many things for different reasons. One thing they did was make objects like this. There are universal elements in this world. When these elements are imbued into something—like a worthless citrine stone, for example—they can become very, very powerful. Like . . ." Diana looked up at Steve. "Like my whip. It's imbued with truth. It's a conduit for the element of truth—that's what powers it. Not me. Truth is bigger than all of us."

Diana looked back down at the inscribed gold ring—all that she had of the elemental stone that Maxwell Lord had taken.

"But what element was imbedded into this stone?" she wondered aloud.

"Love?" Steve asked. "Diana, if this stone is what brought me back, maybe it was love. Or hope."

Diana's heart filled to bursting. She wanted so badly to believe that. She wanted so badly for all of this to be good news—for the stone to be a force for good. For Steve's return to be a blessing, pure and simple. For there to be no darkness linked to this gift.

"Maybe," she said. "It's . . . Steve, it's hard to know. Whatever it is, even if it *was* good, I can promise you that it's too powerful for Maxwell Lord to wield."

Steve nodded solemnly.

"We have to find him. Right now."

EIGHT

We have to get to Egypt," Diana said. "As quickly as we can."

Diana and Steve had found a receipt for a plane ticket in Maxwell Lord's office, and he was going to Cairo. His flight had already left, but if Diana and Steve moved fast, they'd be able to stay on his tail.

"We'll never be able to get you onto a plane," Diana said told Steve as they snuck back out of the headquarters of Black Gold. The sun was setting outside, but the crowd of angry would-be buyers was still yelling and clogging the sidewalk. If anything, there were even more of them now than there had been an hour ago. "You don't even have a passport."

Steve shrugged and gave Diana a cocky wink. "I don't want to *get on* a plane . . . ," he said.

Diana stared at him. Was he really suggesting . . . ?

He was. Steve wanted to fly a plane and pilot it all the way to Egypt . . . himself. Diana opened her mouth to say,

"No, that's a terrible idea," but then she thought about it a bit more. This was an emergency—a potentially world-ending emergency, if she was right about that stone. And she really *couldn't* fly on a commercial airline with Steve. As far as 1984 was concerned, Steve didn't exist.

"Well . . . ," she said. And Steve grinned.

"I knew you'd see it my way," he said.

And that was how Diana and Steve found themselves, just after sunset, sneaking up to a locked security door at a storage hangar attached to the National Air and Space Museum. Diana leaned back and raised her foot, ready to kick the door in, but Steve held out a hand to stop her. He fished a Swiss Army knife out of his pocket and quietly jimmied the door open.

"I don't think lock technology has changed much in the last sixty years," he said, swinging the door open and gesturing grandly for Diana to step through. "Some things still work the same."

Diana and Steve snuck quietly through the hangar. Diana watched with amusement and affection as Steve tried to stay focused on their mission . . . but kept getting distracted by the many, many airplanes from many different periods that were stored in the enormous hangar. "Holy moly," he murmured softly, running his hand along the side of a plane.

"Diana, there's an entire history here," he told her, gazing around as they walked through the echoing space, lit only by the light seeping in the windows from outside. "It's the entire history of aviation—of pilots."

They had emerged onto a darkened runway behind the hangar. A few new arrivals were parked there— cutting-edge military jets packed to the gills with technology so new that most of the world didn't even know about it yet.

Steve let out a low, awed whistle and trotted right toward a huge inky-black jet. It was nearly invisible against the night's darkness. Diana could just barely make out its angular, dangerous lines, limned with moonlight and reflected security lamps. She scanned the runway—all clear. She climbed into the cockpit, and Steve slid into the pilot's seat, practically giggling in excitement. He punched a button, and the dashboard lit up—a dazzling array of dials, switches, readouts, and buttons whose purposes Diana could only guess at.

"Yikes," Steve said. Diana guessed he had never seen anything like it either. But after a moment of total bafflement, he started flipping switches and stabbing at buttons.

"Here goes nothing," he said, and grabbed the control stick. The engines roared to life, and the whole jet started vibrating violently. Diana had never felt anything like it. And the noise was—deafening.

"Go! Get us out of here," Diana said. She didn't need her Amazonian hearing to know that the snoozing security guard had woken up the instant those engines had roared on.

"I'm trying," Steve said, frantically adjusting knobs and flipping switches as he steered the taxiing jet through the dark toward the runway. Just a few more moments and they'd be—

Blazingly bright light blinded Diana. She squinted and blinked, desperately trying to clear her vision. The security lights had come on, and muffled shouts mingled with clanging alarms. They'd been spotted.

Steve pushed the throttle and the jet shot forward, roaring down the runway. A fleet of military trucks pulled onto the runway behind them . . . and another one turned onto the runway *in front of them*. They were going to have to get airborne fast, or else they'd end up mowing down those trucks! Diana clenched her fists helplessly. The jet was racing down the runway faster and faster—but would it have time to get enough speed for takeoff? It had to. They had no choice!

"Get airborne now!" she yelled into the radio.

"Hang on!" Steve yelled back. "Here we go!"

He yanked the control stick up and hit the throttle, and the F-111 roared into the air, its landing gear just grazing the very tops of the military jeeps as it swept over them into the night sky.

As they climbed to altitude, Steve leaned the jet into a steep curve over Washington, DC, and Diana leaned over to look out the window. Lights from a million windows and streets twinkled and glimmered. It was beautiful. This city—*her* city—was beautiful. When you were down in it, it was so easy to get lost in the noise and the smells and the thousand indignities that humankind subjected itself to. But from up here, at night, it was an orderly ocean of lights, a blanket of gems.

And then, as if to mirror the glittering splendor down on Earth, the sky around them lit up in a thousand different colors.

"*What*—" Diana breathed, and then she realized.

"Fireworks," Steve said, staring around them. A brilliant cascade of red and orange shimmered around them, and muffled *BOOMs* resounded through the air as the fireworks detonated just below them.

"But why—" Steve started, and Diana answered as she remembered what day it was.

"The fourth," she said. July fourth. Of course.

"The Fourth of July!" Steve crowed. He smiled in wonder and banked toward the fireworks, throttling the plane back to its slowest airborne speed.

Diana felt happier in that moment than she had for sixty-six years.

Meanwhile, in a basement research room at the FBI, Barbara was knee-deep in microfiche.

She'd been working her way through the FBI's archives all night, but her mind wasn't at all tired, not even after speed-reading her way through thousands of articles, reports, and clippings related to the cache of artifacts that had included that citrine stone.

Barbara was pretty sure she wasn't supposed to be here at all, especially not this late at night. And she was absolutely sure she wasn't supposed to have access to these files. But she'd been *very* charming when she asked, and the FBI agent she'd been talking to had agreed to break all kinds of rules to help her out.

Here he came again. Barbara's eyes flickered up from the microfiche reader. Her helper dropped another stack of films on the table for her. Barbara ignored him as she grabbed the first one and loaded it into the reader. Huh . . . this was interesting. She scanned quickly through images of a recent archaeological dig funded by the Mexican government. "Near-ancient Mayan ruins . . . ," Barbara murmured. And suddenly she knew.

She straightened up. The FBI guy was still there, smiling at her. "Anything else I can get you?" he asked, laying on the charm. "Coffee? Tea?"

Any other time, and Barbara would have enjoyed flirting with an FBI agent. After all, how often did you get the chance? But right now she was on a mission. She had no time for this guy, and no interest in him.

"I don't need anything from you at all," she said plainly, not bothering to smile. She grabbed her bag and headed for the door. "And I'm done, anyway."

"Hey," he said to her back as she left. "You don't have to be so mean!"

Barbara didn't turn, and didn't answer. She was already heading up the stairs. She had an embassy to break into.

The Mexican embassy was several miles from the FBI research archives, but Barbara didn't bother waiting for the bus or hailing a taxi. Instead, she just ran. As she went, her strides lengthened and the blood pounded in her ears. She felt like she could run forever. And she was making better time than most of the cars going by on the avenue.

Breaking into the embassy was laughably easy. Barbara leaped up, reaching for the bottom of a second-floor balcony above the front door and pulling herself up onto it. The knob on the balcony door was trivial to force.

Once she was inside, she made her way through the dark, silent building and found the records room without much trouble. Barbara didn't bother turning on a light before she started leafing through papers. She could read with no difficulty. It didn't take her long to find a file on that particular archaeological dig. And it was full of photos of the various artifacts that had been recovered from it—including the citrine.

Barbara grabbed the file and jumped nimbly back down from the balcony. She didn't bother sprinting this time. She was enjoying the night too much. Ever since that scary guy had tried to mug her the other night,

Barbara had been feeling a little shaky when she was alone outside. But not tonight. Tonight, she felt strong. She felt *dangerous*. And she loved the feeling.

"Hey there," a voice said. And suddenly Barbara realized where she'd wandered on her walk. She was at exactly the same corner as she'd been when that guy had attacked her.

Barbara stopped and spun on one heel. There he was, weaving unsteadily toward her, casting a long shadow in the single light of a nearby streetlamp.

"You talking to me?" Barbara asked, her voice sharp.

"C'mere," the man said, stepping closer. Barbara didn't move away.

"Don't tell me what to do," she said. "How about I tell you instead? Stop harassing people like me."

She stepped into the light so he could see her face more clearly. "Remember me?"

The guy stopped for a moment, taken aback. He obviously *did* remember her, and he also obviously remembered what had happened to him. He looked around.

"I don't see your friend here," he said to Barbara. "Nobody to protect you this time."

And he took another step toward her. Barbara still didn't back away. And she didn't stop smiling. Instead, she took one long step toward him and grabbed his arms. He grunted, surprised, and strained to break her grip. But Barbara held firm. It was—as many things were lately—surprisingly easy.

"Nope," Barbara said. "Nobody but little old me."

She heaved him up and sent him flying into the wall.

Barbara strolled over him, taking her time. He climbed unsteadily to his feet. "Hey . . . ," he said, holding up his hands in useless defense. But Barbara ignored him. She picked him up and punched him, hard.

"Barbara! Are you okay?"

Barbara came back to herself in pieces.

She was in a dark alley. There was blood on her knuckles. Her homeless friend, Leon, was there. Leon looked scared. Leon looked scared *of her*.

Barbara looked down at the man she'd attacked. And then she understood why Leon looked so scared.

What had she done?

"Barbara," Leon said gently. He held out a hand as if to calm her. "Barbara, I'm your friend."

"I don't need friends," she said. She sneered and looked Leon up and down, taking in every tatter, every stain on his clothes.

"Especially not friends like *you*," she said.

Barbara turned and ran into the night.

NINE

Emir Said Bin Abydos was a very powerful man. His ancestral lands in Egypt were once rich with oil, and that had made his family very rich in turn. But over time, much of that land—and the power that came with it—was lost. He was a man who was used to having things his own way. He was a man who was *not* used to surprises.

And meeting Maxwell Lord in the opulent gardens of his personal compound was clearly a surprise.

Maxwell held in a laugh as the emir looked him up and down, scowling at him like he was an unwelcome bug. He was looking at Maxwell the way everyone had always looked at Maxwell, his whole life. Until now, that is.

Until Maxwell's oil fields had struck pay.

And now Maxwell was here for the emir's oil fields. Only the emir didn't know it.

"I must admit, Mr. Lord," the emir said to Maxwell, "I was surprised to see your name on my guest list today.

Seeing as I had never even heard of you until yesterday."

The emir's tone was not friendly. And his security detail—forty or so ex-military men armed to the teeth—picked up on his tone. They edged in a little closer, glaring at Maxwell. Maxwell swallowed nervously.

"Then I appreciate the audience all the more, Your Highness," he said sweetly.

"My advisers are usually very reliable when it comes to vetting my schedule," the emir continued. He began strolling down a long walk lined with roses, and Maxwell followed. "You must be very persuasive."

"I can be," Maxwell agreed. He'd tricked several people into wishes that eventually got him an audience with the emir. It actually hadn't been that hard. Maxwell was getting the hang of leading people to just the right wish. The wish that would benefit *him* . . . and nobody else.

"Persuasive," the emir continued, "and *lucky*." He shot a cold, perceptive look at Maxwell, and Maxwell fought the urge to hunch his shoulders. It was no coincidence this guy was one of the most powerful people in the world—nothing got by him. Maxwell could tell.

"Your good fortune," the emir went on, "has been very impressive, these last few days. So much so that one might suspect it wasn't good fortune at all."

Maxwell said nothing.

"So why come all this way to see me, Mr. Lord?" the emir asked, idly plucking a rose from one of the bushes. He began tearing the petals out, one by one.

"To meet a peer," Maxwell said, in what he hoped was a steady voice.

"A peer?" the emir scoffed. "No, Mr. Lord. You are no peer of mine. But I agreed to see you, nonetheless. Why?" He glared at Maxwell. "I was curious."

"Curious?" Maxwell said mildly. His heart was jackhammering in his chest, and it was taking everything he could manage to keep a calm facade. But he *had* to get this right. This guy was the key to his next move—the move that would put him on top of the world for good. "Curious about what?"

"No one gets that lucky," the emir hissed, leaning in closely. His breath was hot and smelled of anise. Maxwell sweated harder.

"How did you do it?" the emir whispered. Maxwell stared at him. Then he shrugged. *Why the hell not,* he thought. And so he told the emir the truth.

"I lucked into a secret," he said. "The secret . . . *of the wish.*"

The emir didn't even blink. Maxwell kept going. "An

object to grant wishes. And people made wishes for me. I granted those wishes, and I granted more wishes . . . and here we are."

Maxwell leaned in—it was his turn now to invade the emir's personal space. He kept his eyes locked on the emir's and put his hand on the man's arm. "Tell me," Maxwell said very quietly, "what do *you* wish for? Tell me that, and I will show you just how it works."

Minutes later, Maxwell was zooming away from the emir's compound in a caravan of heavily armored trucks. He'd tried to trick the emir into wishing away his oil, only to discover that the man had just sold all of his oil to the Saudis. So Maxwell had seamlessly pivoted and struck a deal: he would grant the emir ownership of his ancestral lands in Egypt.

He had hired a small mercenary army with his new-found riches, as so much attention was now on him.

And it was time to head back to DC.

Diana stared around in dismay. Egypt was in utter chaos. Radios blared the news: a forty-foot wall had appeared out of nowhere, bisecting the country. The wall appeared to trace an ancient border . . . the border of a land that no longer existed. A land that had belonged to the ancestors of Emir Said Bin Abydos.

"What is going on around here?" Steve asked Diana. They were in a cab headed toward the emir's compound. Total chaos reigned in the streets.

"It's Maxwell," Diana said. "It has to be. The power of that stone is creating this chaos."

"We have to find him," Steve said. "And fast."

Diana nodded. At that moment, a military convoy thundered by them in the opposite direction. Their cab driver swerved, desperately trying to stay on the road.

Diana wrapped a protective arm around Steve and braced them against the door with her other hand as the cab nearly veered into a ditch. As she glanced out the window, she happened to see the man riding the back seat of the car in the center of the convoy.

It was Maxwell Lord.

"That was him!" she cried. In Arabic, she asked the driver to follow the convoy.

The driver stared back at her in confusion. Instead of plunging into a U-turn and chasing the convoy, he pulled over at the side of the road.

This guy is not the man for this job, Diana thought ruefully. She rummaged in her purse and pulled out a wad of cash—more than enough money to buy the rusted cab.

"This car, can we buy it?" she asked in Arabic. She stuffed the cash into the cab driver's hands. He took a quick look at the money and nodded eagerly.

Moments later, the cab was peeling back onto the road, now with Steve driving. Diana quickly shucked off her civilian clothes, revealing her Wonder Woman costume underneath. Slipping her tiara on to keep her hair out of her face, she leaned out the passenger-side window.

Steve gunned the engine and pulled up alongside the convoy, passing each vehicle in turn until they got to the one with Maxwell in it. Maxwell looked out of the window, his eyes widening in shock when he saw Wonder Woman hanging out of a rusted Egyptian cab.

"Get rid of them!" Diana heard him yell to his guards. The truck swerved into the cab, forcing it off the road. Steve cursed and fought with the steering wheel, but the little car still ended up in the sand.

The convoy sped down the road, growing smaller and smaller as it got farther away. Steve threw the car into reverse, but the tires spun, helpless in the slippery sand. Diana choked down her frustration.

"I've got this," she told Steve, and leaped out of the car, racing down the road. Steve would follow as soon as he could, she knew. But she couldn't waste any time.

Her feet pounded the road, and her arms moved like pistons. Diana loved running. And on foot, she was faster than most cars. She grinned tightly as she reached the last car in the convoy. Still running, she reached out and gave it a hard push to the right—and the car veered helplessly off the road.

Diana put on a burst of speed, catching up to the next vehicle. Once she was keeping pace with it, she gathered herself and sprang. She landed lightly on the roof of the car.

Her next leap was not so light. She jumped from the roof to the hood of the car, landing as heavily as she could. With a great *CRUNCH*, the engine caved in and the car spun out, useless.

Two down.

Diana increased her speed until she had reached Maxwell Lord's vehicle. Then she leaped onto the one driving next to it.

Lord looked out the window, staring at her in shock. "How did you—" he started, his voice raised over the roar of the road. But Diana interrupted him.

"You're putting yourself and everyone around you in grave danger, Maxwell," she called. "The tool you have is one of the gods'. It's not something a mortal man like you can handle."

She was hoping to get through to him. She was hoping against hope that Lord would nod, pull over, and agree to stop this madness.

But instead Lord turned his face away from her dismissively. And directed his men to drive the convoy straight into the streets of Cairo, which they were fast approaching.

"*No!*" Diana called. At this speed, they could easily hit someone. The city was densely crowded. The streets were narrow. There were innocent civilians everywhere!

She leaped up and grabbed the car, swinging from the side of it as it careened through the streets of Cairo. "Watch out!" she called. But the driver was too distracted by trying to shake her—he wasn't watching where he was going. And he didn't see the group of children in the street ahead, staring in horror at the trucks that were barreling toward them.

Diana leaped out in front of the caravan. She whipped out her golden lasso and swung it through the air, once, twice, and a third time. *WHOOSH!* She used it to snare the kids and then pulled them to safety, out of the path of the caravan. But saving the kids had taken her full focus, and when she looked up, she was dead in the path of one of the trucks in Lord's convoy, which was bearing down on her at full speed. There was no way she'd be able to leap out of the way in time! Diana hunched down and braced for the impact. She was a demigod, sure, but even she wasn't certain she could survive being hit by an armored truck at fifty miles an hour.

WHAM! SMASH!

The truck didn't make it to Diana. Instead, it was T-boned out of the intersection by a little rusted cab hurtling along a side street. Diana looked on in shock as Steve Trevor climbed shakily out of the totaled cab.

They were both alive—but Maxwell Lord's truck had escaped in all the chaos.

Diana shook her head. What a disaster.

"Things are getting bad here," Steve told Diana. They looked around the crowded square. Helicopters buzzed in the air, jets whizzed overhead. And radios everywhere were blaring the BBC World Service. Diana listened with one ear as she climbed to the top of the tallest building.

". . . being called the 'divine wall,'" the BBC reporter was saying on the radio. "It's a truly unexplainable event that now sees Egypt's poorest communities entirely cut off from their only supply of fresh water."

Diana had reached the top of the building. She scanned the horizon. The mysterious new wall towered not far away, bisecting Egypt. On both sides, terrified people were beginning to riot, and bewildered police and army forces were struggling to keep the peace.

Steve scrambled up behind her. He'd found a small crank radio and was tuning in to an American newscast.

". . . an already tense situation is escalating," the American reporter was saying, "as the Soviet Union announces that they will recognize the emir's claim to leadership of his ancestral lands, now abruptly delineated by the divine wall. The United States, a longtime ally of Egypt, has declared its intention to side with the standing Egyptian government. Both sides have made veiled references to their nuclear arsenals as the conflict escalates."

Diana and Steve looked at each other.

This was bad.

Globally bad.

"In other news," the reporter on the radio continued, "bedlam has broken out in most of the developed world, with the shocking news that American businessman Maxwell Lord has somehow come into possession of more than half of the world's oil reserves. The instability in the oil community has resulted in a run on gas, and public riots and mass panic have incapacitated communities in North America, Europe, and much of South America."

Diana was shocked. Maxwell had only gotten his hands on the stone a few days ago, and the world was already on the brink of catastrophe.

"Come on," she said, grabbing Steve's hand. "We have to find a phone."

Minutes later, Diana was pressing the receiver of a pay phone to her ear and straining to hear Barbara's faint voice over the other end of the crackling international line.

"Barbara, it's Diana," she said. "Did you—"

"Yes," Barbara said eagerly. "Well, sort of. I haven't been able to figure out exactly *what* the stone is, but I found historical images of it."

"From where?" Diana asked eagerly. If Barbara had been able to pin down a location, that might provide a hint as to which god had created the stone.

"Well," Barbara said, "that's the weird part. From *everywhere*."

Diana shook her head in confusion.

"It was first seen in the Indus Valley," Barbara said. "Almost four thousand years ago. Then it popped up again in Carthage in 146 B.C. In Kush in 4 A.D. And Romulus, the last emperor of Rome . . . he was *wearing* it when he was assassinated in 476."

Diana stared at Steve in mounting horror as Barbara's words hit home. He looked at her in concern and confusion. *He can't hear what she's saying*, Diana thought. *That's good. I can spare him this news for another few minutes.*

"The last record I found before it showed up on that ship that the FBI raided," Barbara went on, "was in some previously unknown dead city near Dzibilchaltún."

Diana nodded. She'd almost been expecting that. "The Mayans . . . ," she whispered.

"So I learned," Barbara agreed. "Say," she added curiously. "Where are you calling from, anyway? This is a terrible line."

"Thanks for your help!" Diana said, and hung up. The last thing she wanted to explain to Barbara right now was how she'd gotten to Egypt so fast—or why she was there.

Diana set the phone back on the hook and took a deep, shuddering breath. This was bad news—worse news than she'd been expecting.

Beside her, Steve moved a little closer and wrapped a warm arm around her. "What's up?" he asked gently. Diana sighed. She couldn't keep him in the dark, no matter how badly she wanted to shield him from this.

"The stone has traveled the world," she explained to Steve. "To seemingly different and random places. But they all have one thing in common—the Mayans, the Roman Empire, all of them—their civilizations collapsed catastrophically, without a trace as to why."

Steve paled. "You don't think—" he started.

Overhead, more helicopters roared. Screams broke out near the new wall as the rioters began to overrun the military barricades. Diana couldn't leave the country like this. These poor communities needed fresh water. She sprinted toward the wall, a blur of speed and determination.

BOOM!

She had hit the wall so hard, a massive section was now rubble. The divine wall was not so divine anymore. In a second, she was right next to Steve again as they moved quickly toward the car.

"I don't know what to think, Steve," Diana said. "I can only hope I'm wrong."

But she was pretty sure she wasn't. She'd heard enough.

That harmless citrine fake was the Dreamstone—a legendary item of untold power. But it also held a dark secret that Diana was only starting to realize.

And its maker was the God of Lies.

TEN

Wishes, wishes, wishes.

Maxwell's head was spinning. He was back in DC with his new world-class security detail. He was now in control of over half the world's oil. He was probably the richest man alive. But it wasn't enough. It also wasn't easy, or fun. For one thing, there were still crowds of people yelling to be let into Black Gold, yelling to be given a chance to buy into Maxwell's cooperative.

"Ugh," Maxwell said, looking at the teeming mass of people from his office window. They looked like ants. Like cockroaches. He shuddered. "Like I'd want *those* losers in the club anyway. Can't we tell them they're not invited?"

His new assistant, Emerson, shook his head gravely. "No, sir," he said. "The regulators say so. Also, the FBI called, asking for proof of permits for the security team. And the state department is asking about their visas.

Oh, and the tax board called—"

"They'll bury us in red tape!" Maxwell exploded, striding away from the window and wringing his hands. Being rich and powerful wasn't fun at all! It was just bringing him a whole new kind of pain. "It's a conspiracy! Against my success! They're *jealous*."

"And the DC police are here," Emerson finished nervously. "They're challenging the jurisdiction of your security team."

"That's it," Maxwell said, throwing his hands into the air. "There has to be a better way." He looked around his office wildly. Emerson had already made his wish. He was useless. Maxwell strode past him and hurried onto the floor of the main office space of Black Gold. He grabbed a new aide and held him tightly by the arm.

"You," Maxwell said impatiently. "I know *you* wish I could have an audience with *the president*."

"You bet I do!" the aide said enthusiastically.

Nothing happened.

"Wait, did I ask your wish already?" Maxwell said suspiciously.

"Yesterday," the aide said.

Maxwell dropped the kid's arm and looked around. He now had hundreds of employees. But he couldn't remember which of these drones he'd already used.

"God," Maxwell muttered. "This is so tiresome." Doing things one wish by one wish was hopelessly inefficient. What he needed was a way to touch hundreds— millions—of people at once. A way to mass-produce wishes. To touch the entire world and take care of everything once and for all.

But in the meantime, he grabbed another young employee at random. "You," he said. "You new here?"

He was.

Minutes later, Maxwell was striding through the furious crowd outside, his new Egyptian security guys shielding him as he stepped into his waiting car. He had an audience with the president to attend.

The car started moving forward and then stopped with a jerk. Maxwell looked impatiently over his driver's shoulder. They were in the middle of a bumper-to-bumper traffic jam. Maxwell leaned forward and put his hand on the driver's shoulder.

"Don't you wish this traffic would clear up? And that everywhere you drove, the traffic parted like the great Red Sea?" he asked.

"Sure," the driver said.

And that took care of that.

As Maxwell Lord was sailing unimpeded through the otherwise jammed streets of DC, Barbara Minerva was fighting her way through scenes of public panic, trying not to panic herself.

"Go inside," a woman told her elderly neighbors as Barbara walked by. "Go inside and don't come out again. It isn't safe out here. I heard there's a riot on the east side of town. For some reason the streets are full of cows! And the subway has turned into a river of glitter. I know, that sounds fun. But it's horrible."

Barbara hurried away from them. She didn't need to hear more to know that the whole world had gone crazy.

And she knew why.

Barbara wasn't stupid. She had connected the dots from her research, just the way Diana had probably connected them by now. That stone had been the common factor in the downfall of every major world civilization. The stone granted wishes, and the more wishes it granted, the more the world fell apart.

Barbara also knew that Diana was going to go after Maxwell next. After all, Maxwell was obviously the person who was granting all these wishes that were making the world go crazy. So Diana was going to try to stop him. She was going to try to reverse all the wishes.

She was going to try to reverse *Barbara's* wish along with them.

Barbara shrieked in fury as she walked and tore a tree out of the ground by the roots just to vent. She understood *why* Diana would do that. Diana was a *good person*. She wanted to make a *difference* in the world. And she was already extraordinary. She didn't *need* the stone's wishes. Not like Barbara did.

Barbara caught a glimpse of herself reflected in a shop window. She looked sinewy, beautiful, dangerous. She looked like some kind of big cat, the kind of animal that could kill you with one blow and eat you whole. And she liked it. She felt stronger, uncontrollable, and more powerful than ever before. Nobody could resist power like this.

Barbara scowled. She wasn't going to let Diana reverse the wishes. She was going to stay like this—even if it meant stopping Diana herself.

Even in the quiet, cool stillness of her apartment, Diana could hear the sounds of DC tearing itself apart.

She stepped into her apartment and waved her hand self-consciously.

"Well," she said. "Here we are."

Steve followed her in and immediately spotted the wall where she'd hung all the photos of the two of them, and their old friends. Everyone on that wall was dead, now. Except for Diana—and except for Steve.

Steve picked up his watch and turned it over in his hands.

"Diana," he said gently. "I know it's been hard—"

"You don't know," Diana said, more harshly than she had meant to. "You don't," she said again, more calmly. Sixty years of loneliness. Sixty years without Steve. Sixty years of watching the best—the only—friends she'd ever have grow old and die.

"How can the world go on like this?" Steve asked quietly. He didn't explain what he meant—he didn't have to. Diana knew. And she found she couldn't reply.

"Diana," he said, after she'd remained silent for too long.

"I can't talk about this," Diana said. She grasped his arms and stared deeply into his eyes, willing him to understand. "You're all that I've ever wanted. For so long. You're the only joy I've ever had—or ever asked for."

Steve's face twisted in pain, and he pulled Diana into his arms, folding her into the warmth of his embrace.

"I'm so sorry," he whispered into her ear.

They stood there, motionless, clinging to each other, for a long moment. Then Steve sighed. "But Diana," he said. "The world is so full of joys. So full of *people*."

"I don't want *people*," Diana muttered, on the verge of tears. She sounded like a child and she knew it. But she didn't care. "I don't want *people*, I want *you*. What if destroying the stone destroys you in the process? I can't lose you. Not again."

Diana strode into the secret control room in the back of her apartment. The one she'd built herself—the one nobody knew about. She flipped the lights on. It was a windowless room full of monitors, TV sets, radios, seismographs, and other equipment. She scanned a bank of CCTV feeds, tuning in with half an ear to the radio report about her destroying part of the wall to let water in, rioting in Saudi Arabia, and Indonesia's unexpected rise to the wealthiest country in the world. Behind her, Steve entered and gave a low, impressed whistle as he looked around the room.

"What an operation," he murmured. Then: "What is this?"

Diana turned around. Steve was pointing at a large object, swathed in canvas. He lifted a corner of the canvas. Gold glinted from the shadows.

"It's from my culture," Diana explained. "There was an ancient Amazon warrior. One of our greatest. She'd fought to hold back the tide of men so the others could escape to Themyscira. But she was lost to our world. Left behind."

Diana sighed. "I grew up celebrating her image. . . . So, once I came to this world, I sought her out. But I only found her armor."

Diana glanced back at the bank of CCTV screens. Something strange was happening on the highway. Cars were pulling wildly apart. Some of them were careening off the road. One way or another, they were doing whatever they had to do to make way for a single Rolls-Royce.

It was Maxwell Lord's car.

"Where's he going?" Steve asked, coming up behind Diana.

They watched in horror as the car turned off the highway and made its way to the White House.

Diana grabbed her golden lasso and ran for her balcony. But before she could leap off it, Steve grabbed her. "Diana, what are you doing?" he asked urgently.

"I'm going," Diana said. She tugged on her wrist, but Steve didn't let go. "You have to stay here," she told him.

"No," Steve said firmly. "I'm going with you."

"But how—" Diana started, then stopped when she remembered something. A way to get a normal mortal into the White House without any trickery at all.

"I have an idea," she told Steve, a sly smile on her face.

"What?" Steve asked suspiciously.

Diana smiled innocently. "I know someone," she said. She reached for the phone.

Ten minutes later, smarmy Carl from the Smithsonian gala was meeting Diana and Steve at the tour-group door of the White House.

"Diana," he said, with a greasy grin. "What a pleasure."

Diana smiled politely, and Carl launched right into tour mode. "Now," he said as he led them into the building, "I consider myself a history buff, but even I didn't know that these floors were laid by none other than Jan Lincoln! A little-known descendent of Abraham . . ."

Carl droned on, so in love with the sound of his own voice that he didn't notice Diana and Steve sneaking away.

Elsewhere in the White House, Maxwell Lord was being escorted into the Oval Office. He smiled blandly, but his heart was beating a million beats per minute. This was it. He'd made it into the inner sanctum. All the power he could possibly want was his for the taking.

The president was sitting at his desk. He looked up as Maxwell entered the room, but he hardly seemed to notice him. He had the look of a man who was in way, way over his head. *I can relate,* Maxwell thought.

"Everything okay, Mr. President?" he asked. He strode confidently over to the desk and pulled up a chair for himself.

"Yes . . . ," the president started. Then he shook his head. "Something very strange has happened. I could have sworn I was somewhere else entirely, and now all of a sudden . . ."

Maxwell kept the bland smile pasted on his face. He knew what had probably happened—the wish that had arranged for him to meet the president had happened. Most likely, the poor man had been in some briefing or eating a sandwich when all of a sudden, Maxwell's power had zapped him into the Oval Office so they could have their meeting.

The president straightened up, clearly putting the whole thing out of his mind. "Anyway," he said. "Hectic times, as you know. I have a lot on my mind. In fact, Mr. Lord, I'm afraid I don't even know what we were supposed to discuss today."

Maxwell smiled reassuringly. "Exactly that, Mr. President," he said. "These hectic times. And you, our fearless leader, alone at the top. Making hard decisions for the whole world."

The president swallowed nervously. Clearly Maxwell had struck a nerve. And he kept going.

"You're having some troubles," he said gently. "I want to help."

"I appreciate your concern, Mr. Lord," the president said, drawing his authority around him like a cloak. The frightened, vulnerable man who had been confiding in Maxwell had disappeared, stuffed behind the facade of a confident world leader. But Maxwell wasn't fooled.

"You're a man of faith," Maxwell said. "As am I. And recently I have been *blessed*. As you have perhaps noticed."

The president nodded.

Maxwell held out his hands, palms up.

"I would like to share my blessings with you," he said.

As though he was helpless to resist, the president took Maxwell's hands. *Like a moth to a flame,* Maxwell thought. He squeezed the president's hands, hard.

"Now tell me," he said. "What is it that you need?"

The president didn't hesitate. "More," he said. "More nuclear weapons. More than Russia has. Closer to Russia than the ones we have now."

Maxwell blanched a little. He'd grown so used to learning about people's darkest desires in the past few days, but this one took even him aback.

The president gripped Maxwell's hands tighter, pleadingly. "If I just had that, Mr. Lord, then they'd have to listen to us!"

"I can do that, but in exchange I need something from you," Maxwell said. "Please inform your people that I'd appreciate no more interference of any kind. No taxes, no rule of law, no limits. Treat me like a foreign nation with absolute autonomy."

The president nodded. "Done," he said.

Maxwell turned to go. His next move would be to start working on a way to mass-produce wishes. He was done with this one-by-one business. It was inefficient and it was eating up all of his time. He needed to find a way to touch millions of people at once—a way to consolidate his power for good.

As he walked toward the door, he noticed a presentation set up on the side of the room. It showed schematics of a satellite, and an enormous radio dish.

"What's this?" Maxwell asked curiously.

"GBS," the president said. "Global Broadcasting Satellite. A top secret project that would enable us to override any broadcast system in the world. In case we need direct contact with the people of an enemy state."

This is it.

He turned on his heel, facing the president and projecting as much authority as he could. "I need immediate access to this satellite," he said.

Minutes later, he was being escorted by a Secret Service detail toward a helicopter pad. They strode through the halls of the White House. Maxwell was finally going to do it. He was so close—

WHAP!

Suddenly, a glowing yellow cord hissed through the air and wrapped itself around him. Maxwell stumbled and nearly fell, his arms pinned to his sides, his balance thrown off. He spun around and saw—

It was as though the glowing cord allowed him to see two people at once. One of them was Diana Prince, the oddly hostile curator from the Smithsonian. The other, sharing her face and body, was the mysterious crime fighter the news reporters had started to call Wonder Woman.

They were one and the same person.

Maxwell shook his head, dazed. He had to focus. If Wonder Woman was on to him, that wasn't good news. He needed to act, and quickly.

"Come with me," Wonder Woman said. Her voice was stern and authoritative. She was wearing massive, gleaming gold armor. She really looked quite intimidating. "Before you do any more damage."

Maxwell rolled his eyes. "You're one to talk," he said. "But no, I don't think I will."

He turned to the Secret Service agents who had been escorting him. "Remove this woman, please," he said. *"Permanently."*

ELEVEN

Diana took out the Secret Service agents one by one. But then the doors flew open and a dozen more agents flooded in. They raised their pistols and began to fire as well. Diana's grin slipped. This was harder. She spun and leaped, desperately trying to be fast enough. She didn't just have to protect herself— Steve was there with her as well. Her heart pounding, she moved in a blur. One hand still firmly held the golden lasso, with Maxwell Lord tangled up on the other end of it. The other hand was in constant motion as she blocked bullet after bullet.

K-TANG!

Diana looked up in shock. A bullet had been heading directly for her head, and she hadn't seen it, hadn't blocked it.

Steve had.

He was still holding the silver serving tray he'd grabbed

off a nearby table. The bullet was embedded in it.

Diana caught Steve's eye, a moment of stillness in the fight.

This wasn't working. With Diana fighting one-handed, they were outmatched, and they both knew it.

Diana sighed. She hated to release Maxwell Lord, but she had no choice.

She flicked her whip. In one fluid, golden movement, it coiled away from Maxwell Lord and flicked through the room, sending bullets flying. And it sent some Secret Service agents flying too.

Steve tackled one of the agents who was still standing. He knocked the man down and grabbed his gun, raising it toward the other agents.

"No!" Diana cried. "No, Steve! It's not their fault—they think they're doing their duty!"

Steve's face crumpled in frustration, but Diana could tell he understood right away. He threw the gun into a corner. Then he launched himself into the fight bare-fisted, grabbing agents and throwing them into each other. Diana grinned. She loved having Steve on her side in a fight.

Then a large window on one side of the room exploded.

Shards of glass gleamed through the air for a single frozen moment. Then they fell to the ground in a twinkling aura around . . .

"Barbara?" Diana gasped.

It was Barbara. But she was . . .

Different. Altered. She moved like a predator—like a big cat. In her high-heeled shoes, she stalked across the room with sinuous grace. Her fingers were arced in mean curves, like claws. She was wearing a glamorous outfit, but she didn't exactly look beautiful—she looked dangerous.

She made a wish, Diana realized. Barbara had made a wish on the Dreamstone. Diana could only guess what the exact wish had been . . . but this was clearly the result.

"Diana," Barbara said in a knowing voice. She smirked. Diana's heart thumped nervously. Barbara had seen through her costume—she'd connected the dots between Diana Prince and the demigod who fought crime in Washington, DC.

"Diana," Barbara said again, the smile slipping from her face. Now she looked deadly serious. "I can't let you do this."

Diana's heart twisted. She loved Barbara. She'd really connected with her—had finally had a *friend* in the modern world. And now, all of a sudden, they were on opposite sides. *Curse the Dreamstone,* Diana thought bitterly.

But she didn't have time to dwell on the loss. Maxwell Lord had taken advantage of Barbara's distracting arrival and made a break for the stairs one floor below. Steve was in hot pursuit, but Diana didn't want to take any chances.

I'll patch things up with Barbara when this is all over, she promised herself, and then turned away from her friend, running to the staircase and leaping over the edge to land lightly on the landing below. Lord skidded to a halt in front of her, trapped.

Diana grinned tightly. She reached out to finally capture Lord when—

WHAM!

She was flying across the room. Something had hit her—but what?

Diana tumbled gracefully, landing to skid on the balls of her feet. Her fingers just brushed the floor as she steadied herself. She raised her gaze to—

Barbara. It had been Barbara who had hit her. Barbara who had been powerful enough—and fast enough—to send an Amazon sailing across the room.

"What—" Diana said, shocked. "How did you—"

Barbara shook her head and stalked toward Diana. "I can't let you stop Maxwell," she said. "You're not the only one with something to lose here."

Barbara made a gesture that encompassed her whole self—her wild, blank eyes. Her long, rangy limbs. Her suddenly sleek, suddenly glamorous hair.

"It turns out," Barbara said, "that wishing 'to be like Diana' came with some surprises."

Barbara had already been so wonderful—smart, curious, funny, kind—that it made Diana sad to learn that she'd been so unhappy in her own skin. But she couldn't dwell on it now. She needed to fight her friend, and she needed to win. The fate of the world was at stake.

Diana raised her fists. Barbara raised hers in response. And the two women squared off, eyes locked, waiting in tense silence to see who would make the first move.

"Hands up!" a harsh voice cried. Diana's gaze flicked away from Barbara's as she took in the rest of the room. The Secret Service agents she'd been fighting had climbed to their feet and found their weapons, and now a bunch of them were surrounding Diana and Barbara, guns raised.

Diana looked back at Barbara. Barbara was grinning

at the Secret Service agents. There was no mercy in her smile.

Barbara flung herself into the air in a blur of cheetah print and long fingernails, and took out three Secret Service agents before she'd even touched the ground again. The men fell, two unconscious and one groaning, clutching at a broken arm and a slashed face.

I've got to stop her, Diana thought, springing after her friend.

One by one, Diana stood between Barbara and the agents just long enough to give them a chance to make their escapes. It was rough going. Barbara was as strong and fast as Diana, and she wasn't pulling her punches. But eventually the last of the Secret Service agents had fled the room and it was just Diana and Barbara, squaring off again.

"Barbara!" Diana panted, trying once more to reach her friend. "You have no idea what you're dealing with. I'm not what you think. And you can't possibly understand or handle—"

Barbara leaped at her, her face twisted in rage. She struck with the heel of one foot, and as Diana dodged, she caught her square on the jaw with her opposite fist.

"I can't possibly understand?" Barbara shrieked, furious. "Dumb little old me, little old *nobody, nothing me?*
I can't *handle this power?*"

"No," Diana started to say. "That's not—"

But Barbara ignored her. "Well, I *am* handling it,"
she snarled. "I'm handling it *beautifully.* And I am *not
giving it back.*"

She dropped into a crouch, and Diana braced herself
for another attack. But when Barbara leaped, she leaped
straight over Diana's head, and Diana leaped after her.
But she was too slow. She watched helplessly as Barbara
grabbed Maxwell Lord from Steve's grasp and pushed
him toward the door.

"Go," Barbara commanded Lord. "Run. And don't
look back."

Maxwell Lord did as he was told. He fled the room at
top speed. Steve started to pursue, but Barbara yanked
him away from the door and threw him into a wall.

"Steve!" Diana cried, terrified. But he crawled back
up the wall to a stand and flashed her a thumbs-up. He
was dazed but okay.

Barbara stood in the doorway that Maxwell Lord had
used, blocking it defiantly.

"You've always had everything," she told Diana in a

resentful voice. "While people like me have had *nothing*. Now it's my turn, and you're not taking it from me. Ever. And if you try to stop Maxwell, or to destroy the Dreamstone, I will destroy *you*."

Diana clenched her fists. But at that moment, a deafening siren ripped through the air. It was so loud it made Diana's teeth rattle in her jaw—so loud she could feel it in her bones. Her hands flew to her ears instinctively. And when she had opened her eyes again, Barbara was gone—vanished out the door that Maxwell Lord had run through.

Steve and Diana stared at each other in shock and confusion. And then the all-encompassing noise died away, and in the moment of ear-ringing silence it left before it started again, Steve yelled, "Air raid siren!"

The Russians had detected the United States's new nuclear weapons—the ones the president had wished for.

And they were retaliating.

Maxwell Lord was on his way to use the power of the Dreamstone to annihilate the world—if nuclear war didn't take care of it first.

As for Barbara, Diana knew she wasn't stupid. Barbara wasn't going to see this through to the end with Maxwell Lord. No. Barbara was much smarter than that, and her heart was so far gone at this point . . . Diana needed to focus on finding and capturing Maxwell and the stone. Then that would fix everything, including Barbara before she was completely consumed by the stone.

Diana looked down at her hands, then up at Steve, waiting for her with hope and determination written all over his face.

"We are going to find Maxwell," Steve said. "We need his help to stop everything that he has done by granting these wishes."

Diana smiled. "There's a lot of work to do."

All I have is my lasso, Diana thought. *And myself.*

Many lifetimes ago, when Diana was a little girl, she had wept in bitter disappointment in her mother's arms at the Amazon Games. She'd wept because she'd wanted so badly to be a great warrior, but had failed. She'd wept because she wasn't ready, and she knew it. Hippolyta had held her in her arms and stroked her hair, shushing her and whispering the same thing over and over again:

"Your time will come, when you are ready."

Diana stood tall, her golden armor shining. The world was convulsing, thrown into chaos by a con man who had harnessed the worst wickedness of the gods themselves. Two global superpowers were poised on the verge of nuclear annihilation.

But Diana's time had come. She was ready.

And there would be no stopping her.

Diana grinned at Steve.

"Let's go," she said, grabbing his hand as they ran for the door.

She had a world to save.